CHARCO PRESS

Director & Editor: Carolina Orloff
Director: Samuel McDowell

charcopress.com

Loop was published on
80gsm Munken Premium Cream paper.

The text was designed using
Bembo 11.5 and ITC Galliard Pro.

Printed in September 2019 by TJ International
Padstow, Cornwall, PL28 8RW using responsibly sourced
paper and environmentally-friendly adhesive.

MIX
Paper from
responsible sources
FSC
www.fsc.org
FSC® C013056

A NOTE ON THE TEXT

Whenever possible, references to quoted texts were taken from existing translations. Here are the bibliographical details of this cited material, in order of allusion within *Loop*:

Alexander Vvedensky, *The Gray Notebook*, trans. by Matvei Yankelevich, New York: Ugly Duckling Presse, 2002.

Franz Kafka, *The Blue Octavo Notebooks*, ed. Max Brod, trans. by Ernest Kaiser & Eithne Wilkins, Cambridge: Exact Change, 1991.

Machado de Assis, 'The Alienist', *The Collected Stories of Machado de Assis*, trans. by Margaret Jull Costa and Robin Patterson, New York: Liveright, 2018.

Clarice Lispector, *The Foreign Legion*, trans. by Giovanni Pontiero, Manchester: Carcanet Press Limited, 1986.

John Cage, Transcript of story 1: Indeterminacy... *Ninety Stories by John Cage*, in *Die Reihe No. 5*, ed. by H. Eimert and K. Stockhausen, London: Theodore Presser Co., 1961.

Ovid, *Heroides*, trans. by Grant Showerman, Loeb Classical Library, Cambridge, MA: Harvard University Press, 1914.

Clarice Lispector, 'The Smallest Woman in the World', *Complete Stories*, trans. by Katrina Dodson, New York: New Directions, 2015.

Fernando Pessoa, 'A morte é a curva da estrada', *A Little Larger Than the Entire Universe*, trans. by Richard Zenith, New York: Penguin Classics, 2006.

Fernando Pessoa, *The Book of Disquiet*, trans. by Richard Zenith, New York: Penguin Classics, 2002.

Emmanuel Bove, *My Friends*, trans. by Janet Louth, Manchester: Carcanet Press, 1986.

Homer, *The Odyssey*, trans. by Robert Fagles, New York: Penguin Classics, 1997.

the main character, calls in at a pharmacy. There's a man sitting next to the weighing scales. He's so small that the nape of his neck is resting against the back of the chair and his legs are dangling like a pair of tights on a washing line, the toes pointing down. Victor finds him strange; he's taken aback by this man sitting next to the scales. A woman explains: 'Everybody knows him in this district. He's a dwarf. Real unfortunates have pride; they don't draw attention to themselves. There's nothing remarkable about that man: he drinks.' The dwarf on the block, in contrast, was interesting from that first casual smile in the street.

The stories in the ideal notebook may not cross paths any more than rivers do, and yet they're still contained between two red covers.

Maybe I'm not in the middle of the sea, swimming onwards and getting further away, like I thought. Maybe it's the journey, that journey made up of moments. What happens between one instant and the next. What doesn't happen. All those stories, stories that meet and stories that never cross paths. All those moments between two covers. These covers.

This is the ending of *My Friends* by Emmanuel Bove: 'Some strong men are not lonely when they are alone, but I, who am weak, am lonely when I have no friends.' That is, without Carolina, Guillermo, Tania, Tepepunk, Julia, Antonio and Luis Felipe.

I still haven't left because I'd like to tell you here, before you come back tonight, that maybe I won't turn into a bird. It's not the ideal ending, but what can we do. I won't turn into one in the future either, because, however profound or superficial the journey may be, what's trans-formed is the way we recount it. If that's transformed, then everything is transformed. Misfortune, pain, tragedy all ought to be transformed into something else. Maybe that's why we have to look over our shoulder, to turn back so we can be here. Looking at tragedy in order to transform it, so we can be here. Not only be here, but be here properly. Here, in this country. Here, in the apartment.

Change. Unlearning yourself is more important than knowing yourself.

No, I won't turn into a bird. Even though Wild is the Wind, I'm sitting on the same wooden chair as when I began. But then, you can never sit down twice on the same chair twice. No, there's another reason why I won't turn into a bird: I'm not the one that has to be trans-formed. The transformation happened to this story.

LOOP

First published by Charco Press 2019

Charco Press Ltd., Office 59, 44-46 Morningside Road, Edinburgh
EH10 4BF

A CIP catalogue record for this book is available from the British Library.

ISBN: 978-1-9164656-4-0
e-book: 978-1-9993684-1-8

www.charcopress.com

Edited by Fionn Petch
Cover design by Pablo Font
Typeset by Laura Jones
Proofread by Fiona Mackintosh

2 4 6 8 10 9 7 5 3 1

Supported using public funding by
**ARTS COUNCIL
ENGLAND**

LOTTERY FUNDED

Brenda Lozano

LOOP

Translated by
Annie McDermott

CHARCO PRESS

For Diego, Emiliano and Patricio

'For love is ever filled with fear'
Letter from Penelope to Odysseus,
Heroides, Ovid

'Sea, oh sea, you're the homeland of waves,
the waves are sea-children.
The sea is their mother
and their sister's the notebook.
It's been that way now for many a century.
And they lived very well.
And prayed often.
The sea to God
and the children to God.
And after, they resettled in the sky.
From where they sprayed rain,
and on that rainy spot a house grew.
The house lived well.
It taught the doors and windows to play
shore, immortality, dream and notebook.
Once upon a time.'
'The Song of the Notebook', Alexander Vvedensky

'A hundred thousand welcomes! I could weep,
And I could laugh; I am light, and heavy. Welcome!'
The Tragedy of Coriolanus, William Shakespeare

1

Today a dwarf smiled at me.

As a girl I thought the electric pencil sharpener was what separated me from adult life. Between the blue plastic pencil sharpener and the electric pencil sharpener – in my father's office or on the teacher's desk – stretched the distance between childhood and adult life.

At a dinner party when he was twenty-one, Proust was asked some questions. Among them, what his favourite bird was. The swallow, he replied. Proust didn't invent the questions known as the 'Proust questionnaire', but his answers were so good they made the questionnaire famous. Proust responded to the questionnaire on two separate occasions. He was fifteen when he was asked his favourite colour. 'The beauty is not in the colours, but in their harmony,' he said.

At fifteen I still thought the electric pencil sharpener separated me from adult life. If I'd been asked my favourite colour I would have said the colour of my blue pencil sharpener, but Proust's favourite bird is also my favourite bird.

If I could turn into any bird, I'd choose a swallow.

Change. Unlearning yourself is more important than knowing yourself.

Jonás and I did a crossword together this evening. We made a good team. It was a kind of crossword with lots of blank numbered squares. You had to work out which letter of the alphabet corresponded to each number, and then work out the title, the author and the text underneath. He outlined the three-letter words in red, and I outlined the four-letter words in blue. It was a passage from *First Love*, about the love between the character's parents. It took the two of us more than an hour to solve it. Crosswords are a good demonstration of how we function as a couple, in this apartment. A model, on a dwarf scale. His maths PhD came in useful for solving the puzzle. My degree in communication helped me remember the author's surname. From the surname, we were able to work out the rest of the text thanks to Jonás' usual methodical approach to things. Significant that the word 'mother' appeared so many times. Jonás' mother died a week before we met and this very day, Sunday, would have been her birthday. Every time Jonás read the word 'mother' out loud I felt a pang.

Today I saw the dwarf again, the same one who smiled at me in the street a few days ago. This time he was sitting with his back to me, in a little diner. He was checking something on his phone; I think he was reading the news. His feet, the soles of his shoes, weren't touching the floor, and his knees weren't bent. Straight, the legs of the dwarf sitting on the plastic chair.

Tonight we listened to different versions of 'Wild is the Wind' as we lay in bed. Out of David Bowie and Nina Simone, I'd go for Bowie and Jonás would go for Nina Simone.

I've found my combination: a Scribe notebook for a diary and an Ideal notebook for fiction. This is my married couple. Gemini at last become one. Today is a happy day, a day when I came across some dusty, forgotten Scribe and Ideal notebooks in a stationer's on Calle Alfonso Reyes. They were the last ones. Scribe and Ideal notebooks are very difficult to find, but Alfonso Reyes' passion for fictions is reflected in his street. I feel like Alfonso Reyes should intersect with Borges. The two writers would spend the whole time joking around between their streets, but what paranormal phenomena would take place in the stationer's then?

'The Song of the Notebook'. That's the title of the poem Alexander Vvedensky wrote in a notebook with a grey cover between 1932 and 1933. The collection of poems is called *The Grey Notebook*, simply because of the colour of the cover.

A concert of trees and bushes. The wind in the branches: the song of the notebook in its original version. Silence. Listen to that song.

If Jonás turned into a bird I could ask him to let me fly by his side, like in 'Wild is the Wind'.

I'd like to have dinner with Jonás, but today he won't be home. 'I'm having dinner with my dad,' the message says. I called him. We argued on the phone about something stupid. He's going to spend the night there. I wish I'd never said anything.

The dwarf on the block. Today he was wearing a three-piece suit and carrying a tiny cane. In the evening we exchanged glances. I felt a lot like the dwarf, on another scale of life and needing to lean on a tiny cane.

The dwarf, yes, is a dwarf. He's a neighbour. Probably with a voting card. With a love life and a credit history. But then, the dwarf is also an idea. Of someone who lives on another scale, someone who lives among objects that are too large, too heavy or too tall. Someone who lives in a system, a routine, in everyday life. And yet.

Today I went for coffee with my friend Tania. In the Escandón neighbourhood, Calle de la Prosperidad crosses Avenida Progreso. I read the intersections of streets like they're fortune cookies.

Where am I? In a chair, yes, but it feels like the middle of the ocean. I swim on and get further away. I swim forwards, but I go backwards. The beach seems more distant than before.

This evening Tania, sipping her beer, said casually that according to her cousin from Acapulco, if you don't want to drown in the sea you have to swim diagonally. Wait for the tug of the waves and swim not forwards but diagonally.

How do you swim diagonally in life?

I long for the morning when I wake up transformed into a swallow. Now I imagine two swallows holding a ribbon in the air. On the ribbon, the words 'Ideal Notebook' can clearly be distinguished. The swallow on the left is me, and the swallow on the right is the dwarf on my block.

Two people metamorphosed into animals take on the same proportions. The best time to form a relationship with someone is when they change form.

If a metal band metamorphoses on stage at the Foro Alicia, they'll end up as a group of foxes dressed in black. If the university orchestra metamorphoses in the Nezahualcóyotl concert hall midway through a performance, they'll end up as foxes dressed in black. It's a simple equation: x equals metamorphosis. You need to find x to know which animal you'd be.

One thing I don't like about felt tips is their felt tips. I write by hand, and I have small writing. You can imagine how annoying it gets.

On Saturday afternoon Jonás and I went to a gallery opening. We saw a woman there who was more excited about the party than the exhibition. The artworks were just a bureaucratic pretext for the fun. I liked that about her. She was there to have a good time, plain and simple. 'Some people prefer the cracking to the nuts,' Jonás said, about this woman and her extravagant dance moves. Typical Jonás. Sometimes he takes things more seriously than he should. Needless to say, Jonás doesn't dance.

On the dancefloor, I heard someone say that the Most Important Artist in Mexico was there. That phrase, it seems, has the same atomic number as uranium. Some people went over to talk to him. Later, the Most Important Artist in Mexico took a young woman by the waist and they danced psychedelic cumbias. I thought he was a good dancer. Every so often, people interrupted his dancing to engage him in conversation. It's a shame the woman who prefers the cracking to the nuts didn't dance psychedelic cumbias with the Most Important Artist in Mexico. The dancefloor would have gone up in flames.

The secret of those people going over to interrupt the Most Important Artist in Mexico while he was dancing, now that I think about it, must lie in the very word 'important'. In this city, we could form a cult around that word.

We left the party at the gallery and went to pick up a few things for dinner. I thought I saw Oscar Wilde in the supermarket. I once saw Fernando Pessoa choosing fruit at the Thursday market.

Today is Sunday. Jonás is at his friend Marcos' house right now. Here at home, it's a Sunday for puzzles. What came to nothing first, the corny aunt or the corny poetry she liked to read?

A Sunday for making up pointless sayings.

All texts are grey in the dark.
Stories, like buildings and wars, begin with drafting.
Bookkeeper, keep to your books.

And you know what? A notebook can be a Milky Way of letters.

What does ideal mean? The ideal weight. The ideal height. The ideal house, salary, job. The ideal book. The ideal person. To me, the bell they ring when the rubbish truck is coming is ideal: no accident, no disaster, no catastrophe has the good manners to announce its arrival like that.

I'm swimming diagonally, look. It's getting late, why aren't you back from Marcos' house? I'm not going to ask you the Proust questionnaire; I think the Beckett questionnaire would be better. Come and see.

1. Right leg or left leg?
2. Company or solitude?
3. How would you translate the word *lessness* into Spanish?
4. How many times do you suck on a stone before putting it in your pocket?
5. A dark room, a voice speaks to you. What does it say?
6. Your loved ones live in dustbins and you have a single chocolate-chip cookie. How do you share it?
7. A king with a supermarket trolley or a tramp with a cardboard Burger King crown?
8. What do we talk about when we talk about Godot?

One way of turning into a swallow is by writing: I'm a swallow. But can the written word break the silence like a song?

Oh, music. I like music so much. But not the birds' kind. I like music I can sing in the kitchen while I'm cooking, or in the street while I'm walking along. I know what song you have in your head, Jonás. Sing it to me. You're a good singer, come on.

What genre, what kind of music do we like? It's hard to say, if Ovid is the first punk and Ramones tracks are classics. And they are, aren't they, now the internet is our Alexandria and we're all Aristophanes of Byzantium?

Music. It's so good. If I had to pick ten songs out of all the music I know, I'd pick one by Bob Marley and one by Bach. The two of them would sit together on the same list, with the same panache. The songs that are furthest apart would be like strangers who hit it off right away.

Jonás plays the piano really well. He has beautiful hands, long fingers. He's no good at working music out by ear. Most of the time, he plays from memory, but when he forgets something he looks over the sheet music on the piano at his parents' house. His repertoire is what's contained in those seven or ten notebooks with missing pages: his father's favourite pieces. Jonás plays Bach's preludes and fugues wonderfully. If I tried to play Bach on the piano, the part I'd do best would be grunting like Glenn Gould.

The other night, while his sister and I were making quesadillas, Jonás tried to work out 'Wild is the Wind' on the piano. It was a disaster.

What do I do? What's my job? Aside from working in an office, how do I spend my time? I spend my time drawing all sorts of lines. This Sunday I drew a lot of lines like this one:

_____

I drew lines with a blue pencil. Navy-blue lines, about as many as there are ruled on each page. I drew them with my eyes open and with my eyes closed. With my right hand and my left. Now I'm closing my eyes as I write this line. Like letting go of the steering wheel, look how I'm veering off course. Still, you need a notebook if you want to experience all the different kinds of lines a person can draw.

I drew the lines with a blue school pencil. I've realised that lines repeated from the top to the bottom of the page look like waves. To quote the sea:

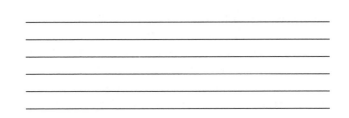

'The sea is the purest and foulest water: for fish drinkable and life-sustaining; for men undrinkable and deadly', I read in a book by Simone Weil. In other words, the stairs that go up and the stairs that go down are one and the same.

It's true, I'm in the middle of the sea. I thought I was swimming forwards, but I'm getting further away. What a strange sensation, thinking you're getting closer when really you're getting further away. Maybe I should ask Tania's cousin for more detail, or enquire on the strip in Acapulco.

There are three thick lines in this Ideal notebook: the sea, the dwarf and the swallow. They're three siblings talking about Jonás. My Jonás. The sea is the oldest, the dwarf is in the middle, and the swallow is the youngest, my favourite. The sea has always been jealous of his sister, the swallow. When they were children, he tried to give her away to the rag-and-bone man.

The rag-and-bone man must have had a Greek equivalent. In some corner of Greek mythology, the original rag-and-bone man drew things towards his cart with the power of his mind.

My Ideal notebook can be an iPod.

An ideal notebook is also a karaoke booth. In its infancy, an ideal notebook can be a drinks coaster, and in later years it can be used to wedge doors open. An ideal notebook of reproductive age opens its two pages even if it's late, it opens its pages even if it's a Sunday morning, like now. An ideal notebook is also a telephone. An ideal notebook allows a Greek metamorphosis to take place in the middle of an office like the one where I work. An ideal notebook isn't written in the third person, or in the first or second, it's written in all three because it's ideal. The same goes for the verb tenses. An ideal notebook can be short, fragmentary, disconnected, long and in-depth, or superficial. It does everything, it allows everything, because Hermes is the almighty father of notebooks.

An ideal notebook has special effects, listen:

A building collapses.
A city crumbles.
The sea parts in two.
A storm breaks.

An ideal notebook knows, above all, that it can't be ideal because being ideal means always being just out of reach – and not right in front of you, Bic pen.

I searched for the Ideal notebook brand online, but I didn't find anything. No photos, no stories. Nothing. Just a mention from a writer saying it exists, that it's the Mexican Moleskine. And as an aside: 'The Ideal brand doesn't have a website.' It's true.

I considered investigating, asking in the old stationery shops around here about the history of Ideal notebooks. I also considered making that history up. A chronology, a chronicle, an oral tradition. Inventing it. Like the *Iliad* of notebooks, from the oral to the written. A long poem about notebooks. The war of the notebooks breaks out between two sides: squared versus lined. The Trojan horse is an HB pencil, and Helen is a beautiful white rubber. The story of Ideal notebooks contains all the elements of an epic poem.

Tonight we had dinner at the Japanese restaurant. He told me they're going away on a family trip, he doesn't know how long for. It will be the three of them: Jonás, his sister Marina and his father. They're going to Spain. His mother was Spanish, she came to Mexico City just before she started her chemistry degree. 'I really want to visit my mum's family,' he said. 'She used to like going on her birthday and this year she couldn't.' It's not *The Iliad* that's beginning now, it's *The Odyssey*. In this story, I'm Penelope. But does that bring me closer or push me further away?

Are these stairs going up or down?

2

'When will you be back, Jonás?' 'I'm not sure,' he answered. I was about to get up. He wrapped his arms around me and pulled me back to bed, and yes, we did it in the morning. Not another line without saying it, I'm going to say it right now: last year I had an accident I almost didn't come back from and not long afterwards I discovered sex with Jonás. Good sex, I mean. In that order.

Sex and love. That order. The death of Jonás' mum. My non-death. That disorder.

I turned thirty. I came early to one thing, and late to another. And now here I am, writing grand words in this little notebook, words like death and sex. But there we go. Later I'll probably explain in more detail. I'm announcing it now like the bell for the rubbish truck.

Shall I tell you something I haven't told you yet? My handwriting is shrinking with time. And now the notebook has shrunk as well. This notebook is smaller than the last one. If there's a miniature scale for people and for notebooks, is there a miniature scale for stories?

I met Jonás through Tania. They were good friends at secondary school. They hadn't seen each other for a while, but Tania was there for him when his mother was dying. A few days after the funeral, Tania invited Jonás round for a coffee. The doctor had said I should go for a walk every afternoon as part of the recovery process. As I strolled along on that sunny afternoon, I thought about how good I felt, how I was completely cured. I decided to buy some mango sorbet and ring my friend Tania's doorbell. Over the intercom, she invited me up. That afternoon, the three of us chatted. Jonás loved the mango sorbet. We moved in together one month later.

Nobody knew if I was going to wake up. I didn't know either. The first thing I heard when I did wake up was one of the nurses singing a Shakira song. One of the nurses pushing my trolley was singing a Shakira song to the other. This can't be death, I thought. I knew I'd come back. Back to life. Back to life and its magnificent vulgarity. Awesome, I thought, here I am. I opened my eyes.

Walking down the street today I came across this Post-it note: 'Marta, a ham and chicken sandwich with no onion. Miguel, a *milanesa* sandwich, all the trimmings, no mayo.' The man who wrote that Post-it probably doesn't like Shakira. Which is a shame, because that song is another great reminder.

Jonás leaves for Spain with his family soon, and I'm staying here in the apartment. With our black cat, our Telemachus.

I said I'd discovered sex with Jonás. Does it relate to what I've been through, or to what he's been through, or to a combination of both? Does it relate to no longer fearing death? Or to our age? What does it relate to, this fact of two people deciding to experiment in ways they haven't before?

Is it possible to stop being afraid of death? I mean, is it possible to stop completely?

This time I searched online for 'an ideal notebook'. I found this question on a forum: 'What would your ideal notebook be?' And the response from a teenager: 'One with a hard cover, and dividers for eight subjects. It would come with coloured pencils, a calculator, a rubber, a pencil sharpener, a ruler etc. You could stick photos on it or leave the cover blue (like the sea).'

I liked this marine parenthesis so much that I brought it over here, like a dog carrying the neighbour's ball in its mouth. And tell me, isn't Mexico located in a kind of marine parenthesis?

You know, Jonás, I was thinking about our conversation at dinner the other night. Phrases and their animal nature. Maybe we could start a zoo, and catalogue the different species of lines.

Lines on the furniture. Invisible lines. Lines of the novels we like and the novels we don't like (yes, in separate cages). Blue lines in school exercise books. Perpendicular and parallel lines. Lines, rows, queues (did I mention that a woman queueing at the bank told me her twins experience all the same things, and that if you hit one the other suddenly gets a bruise?). Metro lines (remember when we were on the metro and you told me how as a boy you tried to run away from home by climbing through the bathroom window?). The line of the equator (this kind of line doesn't exist, but it it's not invisible either. It's a strange category; what do we do with this phantom line?). Bloodlines, paternal, maternal.

Chuy is the woman who cleans the apartment once a week. She's worked for me since before I moved in with Jonás. This afternoon she left me a Post-it on the table: 'Just to say you forgot to buy my bleach again. Kindly buy me my bleach and my green scourers, not the yellow ones because you know the sponges on those don't work, I don't like them. Thank you.'

This morning I read something strange. From my taxi, I read in the window of an occult shop: 'Love makes the ideal real'. I disagree with that window: love doesn't make the ideal real. On the contrary, reality sends us in search of ideals. There's no reverse gear, no opposite direction.

You know what? The government of this country isn't ideal. Today I read a strange fact about Ancient Greece: the statue of Zeus at Olympia was twelve metres tall. The Lighthouse of Alexandria was one hundred and thirty-four metres tall. A building in Mexico City would easily be that tall, or taller. So how tall should the statue be of the president who's left this country with such a horrific death toll?

A call from my friend Antonio. He told me he'd kicked the pavement so hard he hurt his foot. 'Why?' I asked. 'Because someone's car was blocking mine outside my friend's funeral,' he said.

Are there ninety thousand pavements to kick throughout the length and breadth of the country?

Another thing I feel like saying to the window of the occult shop. I'd like to be a tarot card. If I were a tarot card I'd be the lady of pencils, pens and notebooks. Now everything's done on computers, perhaps I could be a saint. The Paper Saint. The Holy Virgin of Stationery. The Xerox Madonna, they'd call me in some offices. Someone would pray to me every morning before putting on his tie.

In my life as the A4 Saint, the Virgin of Stationery, the Xerox Madonna, an office-worker would ask me: 'You used to be an ordinary person, how did you come to be transformed?' I'd answer: 'Look inside your briefcase, my child, and there you will find the miracle.' He'd find Ovid's *Metamorphoses*. He'd be taken aback. With a flash of light, I'd appear before him in a dream and say in an angelic voice: 'Read the book, my child, and you too can undergo a transformation.'

Why this fixation on metamorphoses? Even if we don't turn into animals, we turn into other things. I think that's why Jonás and I are together now, and not sooner.

I can't believe I wrote that someone would pray to me every morning before putting on his tie. But I'm not going to get rid of it. I like the pilgrim life of the Xerox Madonna. Her sandals. Her white dress. Her clasped hands. Her skin as pale as paper. Her blank silence.

Jonás left today, and Marina and his father leave tomorrow. I went with him to the airport. Today I wrote nothing. When I took my pen out of my bag just now I found some receipts. I lined them up in chronological order on the table. The story of my day in receipts.

Today I read nothing. And this, in the whole day, is all I've written.

Third night without Jonás. I feel sleepy. I'm lying in bed.

The cat's in the living room playing with the pencil I dropped; I'm feeling sleepier and sleepier. It's like the cat and I are working shifts on an office reception, taking it in turns behind the desk. I don't know what that means, of course, but it's the kind of thing I write, as if I'm playing with this pencil. Writing is my way of being a cat and shedding fur, or phrases, onto the armchair.

It occurs to me as I'm dozing off that a monument to the dwarf would be no bad thing. A handy reminder of people who live life on another scale. Should it include me? It's true that I go to an office, but do writing and reading exist on another scale in relation to so-called productive life?

I wonder what someone's life would be like if they'd never reached, if they'd never seen, if they couldn't imagine their own depths. Those depths where only pain can take you.

Not long ago I heard a writer discussing death in an interview. He was smoking and laughing sarcastically, with a glass of red wine in his hand. Positively beaming, he said to the interviewer through purplish lips: 'This novel is about death in every respect, and my God, writing it is killing me!' I didn't believe him. You can just tell that the worst thing to happen to this writer in his thirty-something years – aside from a split condom one of the times he's probably cheated on his wife – is missing a flight.

And what if we put up a monument to the writer with a grant?

Holy Child of Grants, look at this glorious procession of grant-holding Young Creators carrying you in a shrine above their heads. So many young people, so many flowers, so many colours. The town orchestra playing the first notes based on one of their projects.

I miss you, Jonás. I know I've told you so many times, but I love your smell, I love your taste. I miss you so much.

I forgot to say that I gave Jonás a notebook like this one so it has a twin. One notebook in Mexico City, another in Madrid. Like the twins of Syracuse. An Ideal notebook I bought for Jonás, identical like a second drop of water, a twin who knows nothing of the other twin's adventures. Perhaps if mine falls over, the other will suddenly get a bruise.

I'm falling asleep. I've gone to bed. I'm more there than here. This isn't very comfortable, let me rearrange the pillow. You know what? If I fold it, it's better. Why am I writing this down? Because this, folding a pillow to make myself more comfortable, is part of the waiting.

3

So is this the story of waiting? *Waiting for Godot*, waiting for Jonás? The difference between Godot and Jonás is that my love really is coming back. Let the music play on!

A family meal. My aunt Eva was visiting from Lisbon. If Jonás were here we'd talk about it in the kitchen, I'd tell him how I planted a lemon tree in Lisbon as a girl. 'Now you have the book and you have the tree, you just need the child,' said my aunt, who never misses a chance to say that by my age she already had two *alfacinhas*. Why are people from Mexico City called *chilangos* and why are people from Lisbon called *alfacinhas*, little lettuces? What do lettuces have to do with Lisbon?

Watch out: I ask questions that aren't real, like plants made of fabric. I'm not looking for answers – questions are more my thing. After all, I like waiting. I like artificial plants like the ones you get in waiting rooms. Not to mention artificial flowers: so pretty. No, Aunt Eva, I'm not going anywhere. This feels a lot like a waiting room, look at these artificial plants and all these artificial flowers. I have a question for you: at what point did poetry become associated with love and rhyming?

At what point did two opposing ideas of poetry – the best and the worst – lie down together in the same bed? Why does the same word mean two very different things? When I say that two words lie down together in the same word-bed, I'm straying into the very worst kind of poetry. There's nothing else for it: I should take up *trova* music.

Oh, *trova*, the bohemian bars. The cafés in neighbourhoods like Coyoacán, Condesa and Roma. A man walks in with his guitar, interrupts the conversation, sings: 'We're two ideas who lie together in the same word, my love; kiss me, take off your dress.' You see the *trovador's* shoes and imagine his bedroom. You imagine his faded bamboo blinds, his ashtray, his mountain of cigarette ends, his cheap wine in a mug with no handle.

As I'm writing, a plane flies overhead. Planes in the background could be seen as a kind of poetic metre. Planes are also a metronome. And as I write this I look at my shoes and see the shoes of a *trovador*. I ought to buy myself a cape. Pass the guitar.

A miracle: it's started to rain. Plus, less miraculous, the neighbour is hammering on the wall. Storm and neighbour. Is the neighbour a domestic version of the storm? Storm, neighbour. Two words in height order, from largest to smallest.

Today I thought about buying wool and knitting needles so I can knit and unravel while Jonás is coming back from his trip, but then I thought that writing in this notebook is a bit like wool, because the lines are baby blue and the words, added in cross-stitch, could even become socks or a scarf or a doily, and maybe I could unravel it all and then knit it and unravel it again while Jonás is coming back from his trip.

I love you, Jonás. I know you know that, but I wanted to remind you, like with a Post-it note.

At work today I accidentally typed alphabert instead of alphabet. If we have a child, we can call it that. As my Aunt Eva says, now I have the tree in Lisbon and the books I publish at work, all we're missing is Alphabert.

My Aunt Eva can be a bit much, but it's true, I did plant my lemon tree with her when I was a girl. I'd forgotten that. Three or four times when I was a teenager she sent me photos of the tree, which was growing taller and taller, with little notes written on the back. I remember one time she wrote in the voice of the tree. 'Look how big I am,' it said on the back of the photo, as if the tree itself had sent me a postcard.

Another plane flies over.

This week I didn't see the dwarf on the block. This week I thought how my notebook is like an armchair and I'm like a cat curled up in it. And this week I forgot to write that on Sunday, before Jonás left, we were driving to the cinema and saw a shop selling tiny furniture. Made-to-measure furniture, the sign said. And in the window there was indeed some made-to-measure furniture. A living room on a smaller scale. 'Look, my love, it's like the seven dwarves' living room,' Jonás said.

I want to kiss you now.

Here come some fabric flowers: it's not that Cato was in favour of lost causes; he himself was a lost cause. Is this something he shares with Kafka? In that sense, Cato is the father of notebooks, and Kafka is one of his brilliant children.

Speaking of Kafka, have I told you he's one of the authors I read for self-improvement? Today I underlined this phrase, which I could repeat every morning: 'He who seeks does not find, but he who does not seek will be found.' In fact, the genre people call self-help literature sounds tautological to me; I read all literature as self-help.

In the car on the way to the airport, we heard a song on the radio. Jonás turned it up. 'This is so good,' he said. I managed to find it later, and I've listened to it quite a bit this week. Now I'm going to turn it up. I hope the neighbours like this song as much as I do.

My dear friend Tepepunk gave me *The Alienist*, by Machado de Assis. I've been reading it all afternoon. There's a minor character who nowadays seems hard to imagine: the rattle man. Before the internet, before the printing press, there was rattle man, who was hired to roam the streets of the town with a rattle in his hand. 'From time to time, he would shake the rattle, towns-people would gather, and he would announce whatever he had been instructed to announce – a cure for fever, plots of arable land for sale, a sonnet, a church donation, the identity of the nosiest busybody in town, the finest speech of the year, and so on.'

If I instructed the rattle man to announce something, it would be a soppy poem. A love poem, with rhymes and flowers, preferably wild flowers. Dedicated, obviously, to Jonás.

Oh, I'm just like all the literature I most despise. Although I do own good books, any bad poem resembles me better.

A seven-hour time difference and the sea in between keep me from sleeping at his side. My ideal notebook, which can do anything, will let me sleep by his side in the land of dreams. By the side of the golden tree which isn't the one I planted as a girl, though it looks a bit like it.

I'm writing this to make it official. My notebook: my guitar.

You carry a notebook identical to this one, you jot down numbers, addresses, the name of a restaurant, the title of a song. I know because, when we don't have them open, your notebook communicates with mine; they're connected by a string like two styrofoam cups.

What made Jonás do a PhD in maths? Was it something to do with his parents, with their jobs – she's a chemist, he's a physicist – or with the fact they met in the seventies, at the piano recitals in the university physics institute? I feel like Jonás is following proudly in his parents' footsteps. Now, for example, he's in Madrid, perhaps walking down the very streets where his mother used to walk. I feel like I'm wandering aimlessly, or in the opposite direction to my parents' footsteps. My parents begot two children: No and No.

My brother lives in London. He's twenty-seven, the age some rock stars died. Jonás' sister lives with their father. She's thirty-three, the age The Rock Star died. I'm in between their ages, but I'm with you in Rockland.

An ideal notebook should be waterproof, like the books children read in the bath. You can't have a notebook getting wet as you wash, like Ulises Lima's books do when he reads in the shower. An ideal notebook should be able to go underwater. Whether it floats like a rubber duck or swims in the deep like a whale, it needs to be waterproof.

Is this glass of water the dwarf-scale sea between us?

4

The dwarf on the block has a three-piece suit, a black bowler hat and a cane. Black shoes polished until they gleam. You could say he's also the most elegant man on the block.

The dwarf, who's a different height, who can sit in a chair and not touch the floor with his shoes. Who lives on a different scale. Who lives in a strange sort of margin. Who has the same abilities as you. Who walks down the same pavement as you. And yet.

Are there dwarf animals? Dwarf giraffes? A panther, a hippo, a bird? A dwarf landscape? There are dwarf planets. You told me that, Jonás. Maybe now I can tell you a story.

Once upon a time there were seven dwarves who sang in the forest. Doc, Grumpy, Happy, Sleepy, Bashful, Sneezy and Dopey. The seven dwarves in a row, from Doc to Dopey. Dopey is a little dwarf. Maybe he's just a little dopey.

Meanwhile, deep in the thick, dark forest, a voice thunders from the top of a castle: 'Mirror, mirror, on the wall, who is the fairest of them all?'

The seven dwarves arrive home and ask in unison who's asleep in the bedroom. They think a monster has got in.

The monster is sleeping across three beds. They want to kill it before it wakes up. Grumpy says: 'Ha, she's a female and all females are poison! We have to get rid of her.' She wakes up, and the seven dwarves duck out of view. 'I wonder if the children are back,' says Snow White. She's scared when she sees the seven little faces. 'Why, you're little men!' 'We're as mad as hornets,' one replies. 'Can you make dapple lumplings?' 'Apple dumplings!' the other six shout back at him. 'Yes,' says Snow White, 'and plum pudding and gooseberry pie.' 'Gooseberry pie?!' the dwarves cry in unison. 'She stays!'

Not unlike tramps in a stage play, with that jolly little dance as they walk, draped in rags, the smudges on their faces meticulously added with make-up: that's how they are in the cartoon. The seven dwarves have hats, white beards and red noses. They're tubby, they sing in unison. The dwarf on the block has a cane, a sober demeanour. Grumpy's anarchy consists of not washing. I imagine the dwarf on the block has voted for the left for as long as he's had a voting card, in the hope that the path we're on might change.

What would the ideal politician be like?

Instead, we're stuck with cartoons. And they do so much harm.

I remember there's a point in *Waiting for Godot* when the characters swap hats again and again. A bit like politicians.

I wonder. What do I wonder?

I miss you, Jonás. I'd sleep with you tonight on those three little beds.

Today, among other things, I bought a kilo of red apples at the market, thinking of Snow White. I thought I spotted the same Fernando Pessoa I saw a while ago at the fruit stall.

Jonás said he broke up with his ex because she didn't like him not having an office job. 'But you teach, you're doing a research project at the university, doesn't that count?' 'It wasn't really about the office,' he went on. 'It was her way of implying she wanted to be with a different sort of person.'

Mirror, mirror, on the wall, who is the fairest of them all?

In the first months of our relationship, I was plagued by the idea that they might get back together. That she might turn up again, that he might want her back. I had no basis for thinking it, I just didn't want things with Jonás to end. I think it's the first time I've ever got on so well with anyone. You could say that, as well as the sex, I've discovered a good friend. I don't know if one is more important than the other. I don't think so.

I like you so much, Jonás, that if you give me the first letter of your name I'll do a magic trick. Pass it over; I'm going to shrink the first letter of your name. Look. A small letter in the world of capitals, and yet it's still a capital. In small caps, a capital letter the same size as the small letters – a dwarf letter?

It's five in the morning. I've just come back from Tepepunk and Nina's. They've been awarded a residency in Tokyo and we were celebrating. We started in a cantina. Now I'm wasted. We were drinking mezcal. Damn mezcal, that cursed happiness. I want to whisper in your ear that I love you. I don't want to go to sleep. I'll give you a letter of the alphabet. Whichever one you want. Kiss me. I love you, choose any letter you like: dkrisncpolñsmciryaxnlñpqoesj.

I've realised that the ideal notebook, like a 7-Eleven, never closes its doors.

I've also realised that when I talk about you, the things I write are like a craft project. I could write this with glue and alphabet pasta. Will it be long before you come back? I hope not. I hope the whale lets you go soon, my Jonah, because I miss you. I'll say it with blue glitter.

Jonás and I are about the same height. Our notebooks are the same size. This makes it easier for the notebooks to have sex.

Tall people who need made-to-measure clothes. Fat people who need double seats. Neurotic people who need positions of power. Stupid people who need someone even more stupid next to them. Insecure people who need the approval of strangers. Loyal people surrounded by traitors. People who don't fit, people who live on another scale.

So what would be a normal scale? What's the median, what's the average, what's 1:1?

A job, an apartment with a mortgage, a car with a payment plan, a family, two boxes of cereal (one high-fibre for mum and dad, and one with chocolate for the kids). A dog needs a lot of looking-after, a kitten would be better and never mind if it gets run over, honey, because we have each other, now go on, put the dwarves to bed because there's school in the morning.

Meaning that being thirty-one and waiting for Jonás to come back from his trip, plus a cat, some plants, some books and an apartment aren't the average.

Let's open the phonelines instead. The ideal notebook is inclusive, with you, and you as well, sir. In this gameshow, *A Hundred Mexicans Said*, here in my ideal notebook. Good evening, we asked a hundred Mexicans if they'd prefer reading or a hamper containing two bottles of cooking oil, tins of tuna, rice, beans, packets of soup, a good selection of biscuits, four bottles of table wine, a delicious cake and none other than the Golden Membership: a year's supply of free food.

If you're one of the hundred people surveyed who don't feature in the most popular response, don't worry – I hear there are biscuits at the end of book launches.

Biscuits. So do we all like biscuits? Biscuits are our unifying thread. We live in the biscuit brotherhood.

Here in Mexico City there's a monument called the Estela de Luz. The Suavicrema, it was nicknamed, because it looks like a Suavicrema wafer. The biscuit elevated into a monument, a biscuit costing 1,575 million pesos. There's no need to do the calculations, the biscuit encapsulates the situation: the millions are shared between a select few, while the snake eats its own tail for money.

And what about education, man?
I can't hear you, man, the music's too loud.
State education, what about it?

What? I can't hear you, man, speak up, the music's amazing. It's wicked, what track is this?

Wild is the Wind. A country shaped like a leaf, about to fall from the tree.

I got distracted. That's what happens when I leave the windows open. But I wasn't distracted enough. You can always go further. Fall out of bed, fall off the Earth, fall into space, into a planetary model, a smaller scale, a styrofoam Pluto. Because Pluto is a dwarf planet. What's a dwarf planet, Jonás? 'Dwarf planets have different characteristics, for example they don't orbit like other planets because their gravity doesn't work the same way. Pluto used to be considered a planet, but not any more. So the science is being rewritten, and now it's considered a dwarf planet. Science has always been like that; it's constantly being rewritten.'

Not having the same kind of gravity, not being part of the average. Is it comedy or tragedy? Can genres be rewritten?

Why the fervent desire to be part of the norm? How to get away from it? What's the most distant point? Where could I go on this wind, on these wings? Oh, the wind, I just love it. How it messes up my hair; how far it can carry me. But am I getting further away or am I getting closer? Where am I going?

Do these stairs go up or down?

I'd like to fly far away, by Jonás' side. When I write I try to distance myself from here. But Jonás isn't the furthest point. Nor is the past. Not even going back to the fall of

Tenochtitlan and the foundation of New Spain would be very far. Imagination is all that can carry us far away, and the fewer pieces the jigsaw has the better. The furthest I can go for the moment is into the cat's head. The sleeping cat, a dwarf panther, here by my side. The cat's so charming when he's asleep. For each battle embarked on by Telemachus, the cat yawns.

I once heard a novelist criticising people who write to the sound of their cat purring when people in the north of the country can hear gunfire. My cat, who sometimes chews books, wonders: aren't books all a similar height?

Isn't literature somewhat misshapen compared to the news? Isn't a novel a kind of dwarf compared to a newspaper? A question of height, a novel next to a printed newspaper: one small, the other big. Then don't writing and reading mean living on another scale without it mattering where you are when you write, with made-to-measure furniture, made-to-measure clothes, while some of the most common verbs in the headlines are abuse-torture-kill?

Literature in this country: a pot-bellied dwarf, red-nosed, in a little red hat. Books are so tiny compared to the horror. Literature in this country is only fit to decorate the garden. He's so elegant, the dwarf on the block, and everything around him is so fucked up.

5

I was in a good mood until I read my horoscope: 'You've realised by now that you're not indispensable to anyone.'

Jonás is a Libra, and I'm a Gemini. Libra is my rising sign. I was told this by a woman wearing blue eyeliner. 'Libra and Gemini are air signs,' she said. The same woman did a tarot reading for me: 'All the cards show you're a double air.' A double power. Wild is the Wind. Does that explain the way I drift from place to place?

If Jonás were here we'd have dinner in the Japanese restaurant a few blocks away. One of our customs, one of our favourite restaurants. The things we like. Oh, it feels so good to hear it in his voice, to hear that plural, which, along with the bed, is too big for me now he's away.

By the way, I listened to another version of 'Wild is the Wind' as I was doing the washing-up. It's great. A good song is so flexible, you can make endless new versions.

Tania called. After a while she said our phonecalls could be an AM radio show in the early hours.

I asked Jonás about scales in science: 'For example, the nanometric scale makes things more reactive than they are at a normal scale, because the atoms it reveals can be used in more ways. Nanotechnology is exciting because it gives things more attractive properties than the properties we're used to.' In other words, today I ate a red apple, but on a nanometric scale the apple would taste better. I asked him some questions about that. Later, I got this message: 'Forget it, my love, you couldn't have a planet revolving around you because of the mass. One mass attracts the other mass, think of Newton's second law. Forget the example I gave of the Smurf revolving around Gargamel.'

Meaning that something on another scale has different characteristics. Its gravity changes. This applies both to the dwarf on the block and to literature.

The ideal is always bigger or smaller than reality. The ideal is on a different scale.

Example: Jesus Christ is the notebook, God is the ideal. Because Jesus Christ came down among men, but we conceive of God as an idea.

Am I the idea I have of myself?

One advantage of the ideal notebook is that it can come with me in the taxi. This is one of its nanometric properties. The taxi driver, an old man with a hearing aid, must think I'm making a note of something for work, something I have to do, something I want to remember in the airport. He watches me in the rear-view mirror. But no, mister, it's not that. I like you, that's what I'm writing. I wish I could tell you. But because I don't dare talk to you, I'll tell you here that the radio station you have on, which is playing *bolero* songs, is the same one my granddad used to listen to. Maybe your shared musical tastes would have given you something to talk about. I don't dare interrupt now you're singing under your breath, but I wish I could tell you that I'm happy you're singing, I like your eyes behind your thick lenses in the rear-view mirror, and how you drive with both hands on the wheel; you've also made me like this song even more. Science is right: notebooks that are smaller in size have more attractive properties than the properties we're used to.

We drove past a bakery called *Esperanza*. Hope. My notebook's name is better than the bakery's. How deep can you swim in the word hope? I think it's a word you can see to the bottom of, like the bottom of a swimming pool.

Opposite me in the waiting area, a fat woman in pink jogging bottoms takes an equally fat pink wallet out of her bag. If that woman were to turn into an object, it would be that fat pink wallet.

Through the aeroplane window I watch as night falls, and it looks so similar to the dawn. In the same way as elderly people end up behaving like children.

So, do the stairs go up or down?

Mexico City from a height. Clarice Lispector says the mirror is the only invented material that's natural. I was born in Mexico, in that word reflected over and over: in Mexico, in Mexico City, in the Hospital de México, and when they were younger my parents lived in an apartment on Calle México. The plane is taking me to a conference for publishers and writers from Mexico.

The organisers ask us not to leave the hotel: 'Please, everyone, things are very dangerous at the moment. We don't want anything to happen to you. All the conference activities will be in the events hall, on the ground floor, next to the lobby. Breakfast, lunch and dinner will be in the buffet, don't forget.'

We're having beers on the balcony of room 401. We're a bit drunk, and meanwhile one girl is sipping fizzy grape-fruit juice with no ice. She talks about the thesis she's writing. She mentions Alberich. I move closer, trying to be casual, and hear: 'a chapter on Alberich the dwarf, the one who guards the Nibelung treasure under the water'.

This morning, in the hotel restaurant, a waitress was humming that Shakira song, the one I think of as a kind of Post-it. That reminder, always so timely. Hearing it put me in a good mood.

From the whole afternoon at the conference, I have three sad postcards. A poet with a centre parting and limp eyelashes blinks slowly, putting on a deep voice to read one of his recent poems. A charmless fiction-writer who reveals his insecurities – that feverish pursuit of acceptance – with everything he says. And Robin syndrome: someone always wanting to be next to Batman (the acclaimed writer or the festival organiser or the superstar publisher).

I asked Jonás over the phone if he thinks poets in all languages put on a different voice when they read their poems out loud. 'I don't know,' he said, 'but it reminds me of that poem you showed me once, by the poet who made lines, zigzags, waves. There are some poems you can't read out loud, my love, and those ones are the most like certain conclusions of physics. The points where poetry and science meet. Science often reaches Dadaist conclusions, you know. Poetry and science at those twin points can't be read out loud.'

There are various signs in the hotel foyer. One of them says it's forbidden to enter with balloons. No smoking, no pets, no inflated balloons. A friend points that sign out to me, puzzled. 'It's not what you think,' says one of the organisers. 'If a balloon bursts in here, we all fall to the floor thinking there's a shootout.'

Drinking beer on the same balcony, with the good news that someone's got hold of some mezcal and plastic cups. We'd all been at a terrible reading, of a terrible book. Someone produces the book. Another person reads passages out loud, imitating the author's voice. We revel in the endless stream of sexual metaphors. It's like the fount of all bad poetry, a great feast of it, or something.

Jonás has gone to Lisbon with his sister, and their father has stayed in Spain with a cousin of their mother. This morning I got a text message: 'Luckily we ran into your granddad, he says what are you on about, you're wrong, the bookshop you recommended isn't there any more. He took us to eat those famous custard tarts, which were really good, by the way.'

Now that I think about it, sexual metaphors are astonishing. Especially bad metaphors, astonishing like the bearded lady's circus act. Bad poetry is astonishing because it's so monstrous. It has all the features we recognise, and yet that hypertrichosis too.

Today I talked to two poets, one bad and one good.

Maybe some company is better indoors and some is better outdoors. A bad poet might be good company in the street, but in a living room what you want is a nice long conversation. There are exceptions. My friend Luis Felipe is a good poet, and you can talk to him both in the street and at home. So the previous assertion should be taken as another artificial plant and my comment about Luis Felipe as an artificial flower.

I came back to my room to read for a bit. I found this from William Hazlitt: 'All that part of the map that we do not see before us is a blank.'

Is the violent part of the map a blank?

Mexico City, seen through the aeroplane window, is bigger than the ball of plasticine a child has just squashed onto the map of Mexico this evening. We make the world to the measure of our hands. But everything has a scale.

Violence has scales.

Any drawing, painting, photograph, lithograph, any picture of a bird, small or large, however rough the likeness, conveys the idea of freedom. Birds are a symbol of freedom.

An open notebook is also a symbol of freedom.

There's a bird on the Mexican flag. The eagle devouring the serpent. I wonder if the flag contains any clues.

'Fly away with me.' If I could turn into any bird I'd choose a swallow. Have you noticed that swallows normally form pairs, Jonás?

Now I'm one of those planes we hear from the apartment on Sunday nights, now I'm flying over the city. From up here it doesn't seem like Wild is the Wind. Instead, Mexico City looks so docile. And the country looks so docile, too, on the map on the aeroplane screen.

6

We argued on the phone.

It's hard for me as well, Jonás. Believe me. I never met her. I'm trying to support you from here. Through you, through your dad and Marina, I love her too. Believe me. If I could do something I would. Believe me.

I'm going to try something. Let's see if this notebook works. Ana? Ana, can you hear me?

Ana. Ana, dear Ana. I love your son. I would have liked to meet you, to call you on the phone, to chat. Really? Me too. Of course, I would have brought you a book. Yes, absolutely, we'd be in the kitchen. Jonás tells me it's the place you like best. I like being there too, it's beautiful when the afternoon light comes streaming in through the big windows. We had lunch in there last Sunday. Yes, Rosario has it all under control. There are often containers of food in the fridge from the day before. I've learnt some of your recipes from Rosario. By the way, the Catalan crème brûlée we had last Sunday was delicious, how do I make it? Thanks, I'll have a look in the drawer. The house is tidy. Marina's really well. Relaxed and well. Yes, all good with him. Jonás – Jonás? Honestly, I don't know. I think he's afraid of being abandoned. But how can I explain that you didn't abandon him? How can I explain that I'm not about to leave him, that I don't want to leave him?

Do you think I could go anywhere?

Where?

Am I getting closer or am I getting further away?

Do these stairs go up or down?

7

This evening, walking down the grassy central reservation with my headphones on, I listened to the David Bowie version of 'Wild is the Wind' and had a metamorphosis. I started to sing, and all of a sudden my voice faltered. I felt an itching in my shoulders. Feathers were sprouting from my arms, my feet stopped touching the ground and at the same time I got smaller. I turned into a swallow. I flew over the grass and across the road. I looked down at the trees and the traffic lights; I saw the office windows and power cables from above. I flew over the park. I looked down at the patios, the cars, pedestrians dotted here and there. I flew over the trees and through the branches, I saw a parked rubbish truck, I paused on a nearby cable. And what if tomorrow I wake up transformed into a person? I love flying. It doesn't mess up my hair, and my feathers suit me perfectly. It feels so good to fly. And oh, I can go so fast. I love being a swallow, I really do.

8

I like this notebook because it's lined. Now and then I think the blue lines are like shelves in a grocer's, somewhere to display all the words heaped haphazardly on the floor. It's eight a.m., time to raise the shutters of this shop. Good morning.

The word of the day, according to the online Oxford Dictionary, is Hikikomori: '(In Japan) the abnormal avoidance of social contact. Japanese origin, literally "staying indoors, (social) withdrawal".'

Dear Oxford Dictionary, Kafka wants to argue back: 'There is no need for you to leave the house. Stay at your table and listen. Don't even listen, just wait. Don't even wait, be completely quiet and alone. The world will offer itself to you to be unmasked; it can't do otherwise; in raptures it will writhe before you.'

I read this article in the paper: 'The British police apologised today after one of their officers shot a blind man with a taser, having mistaken the cane he was carrying for a samurai sword.'

Last night I saw an infomercial I thought was funny, and I told Jonás about it. I realise the word 'infomercial' doesn't appear in the dictionary of the Royal Academy of the Spanish Language, but it does appear in the Oxford Dictionary. I don't share the Spanish linguistic authorities' contempt for the word 'infomercial'. The Spanish economy has the same problem as its dictionary: it's as inflexible as a broom handle. Latin America is the future for Spain, just as it was in the past. Among other things, because we have the word 'infomercial'.

Do they wear ecclesiastical robes when choosing which words to include in the dictionary?

I've finished work. I'm on a bus back to the apartment. A woman on the radio says that a bishop has carried out more than seventy thousand exorcisms in his long career, and that there's a branch of the Vatican which looks after paranormal matters. A bishop in Mexico receives between fifteen and twenty calls a day requesting exorcisms, the woman continues. A big controversy in the Vatican: is it possible for the Pope to carry out an exorcism? The lines are open. Now a *trovador* is singing on the radio. What a terrible song. God bless the nurse who sang Shakira.

I read the top corner of a cargo lorry: 'Don't like how I'm handling this vehicle? Complaints to 5286 8738'. A truck drives past: 'This vehicle is protected by satellite'. On a green post, a sign: 'Wicker furniture repairs'. Travelling home, I read some of the signs and write them down here. Don't like how I'm handling this notebook?

Now I'm writing as I walk. Incredible, isn't it? The ideal notebook could have its own infomercial.

Sir! Madam! Overdoing the hikikomori? Sick of being cooped up indoors reading? Tired of the British police mistaking your cane for a samurai sword? Have you lost faith in the Oxford oracle? Overworked your writing in your creative writing workshop? Do you write novels you think are shit, compose prose you think is crap? How many balls of paper do you throw in the bin without managing a single line? Then it's time to buy an ideal notebook! To hell with Second World War novels, sir; to the devil with historical fiction, madam; forget all those stories about middle-aged European men. Plots come and go, action is secondary. The voice is what matters. Listen to your voice, however it sounds. Practise in the bathroom. Jump up and down a bit first. A-E-I-O-U. Practise in your notebook. 1, 2, 3, 4, 5, 6, 7. Do it again, only this time with your words. One word after another. You don't need to move from your kitchen, all you need is a chair and a table. In fact, you only need the notebook. Dare to pick up that pen.

This afternoon I saw the dwarf in the distance, walking with his back to me and holding his miniature cane. That cane wouldn't have been mistaken for a samurai sword. Maybe for some nunchucks.

Silence and distance, do they bring us closer to the people we love or take us further away?

At the market, I saw Pessoa in the distance. I remembered his phrase: 'It is not love but love's outskirts that are worth knowing'. Waiting is its outskirts; maybe that's why it's worth knowing.

The father of Ernesto, my ex-boyfriend, died when we were living together. I think his father's death brought us closer. Why is your mother's death pushing us apart, Jonás? Why such a long trip? In the apartment Ernesto and I shared, we had an electric oven where we made toast. Huddled around that little oven, we talked a lot about his father. Why aren't you coming back? Why won't you try talking about it?

Guillermo and I left the cantina at three in the morning. The chairs were upturned on the tables. We were drunk, we were the last people there. He walked back to my apartment with me. In the middle of the street, he started to dance something he called 'The Glitter Dance'. With his two index fingers pointing upwards, Guillermo sang, 'This is the glitter dance, ding-ding-ding-dang-dang-dang'. I couldn't copy his moves because I was laughing too hard. We were both laughing, without really knowing why. Eventually I was laughing because he was laughing. Lying in bed with the lights off, I remembered and laughed some more. This morning he sent me a message: 'I'm hungover, take me to the market for some tacos, ding-ding.'

It's Sunday afternoon. I've spoken to Tania, Julia and Carolina. My friends know each other, they say hello if they cross paths, they speak every now and then, but they don't hang out together. I see them separately. This morning I saw Carolina. She gave up coffee when she got pregnant, so she had a juice in the café instead. I had lunch with Julia, and Tania called just now. I've been friends with the three of them since we were teenagers. We didn't go to the same school, I met them in different contexts. Tania is an artist. Julia runs a film festival and plays the guitar pretty well, though she's a bit shy about it. Carolina studied literature, and now she writes and has a small press. I don't go to a psychologist, but if I have any kind of case history, you could say it's in their hands.

The first story I wrote in primary school was about a

giant, and now I'm writing about a dwarf. As a girl I had big handwriting. The two lines in my exercise books were like the floor and the ceiling, and my handwriting was like Alice, squashed uncomfortably between them. Over the years, my handwriting has shrunk. As if every so often it took a little of the blue potion. Maybe that's why I feel closer to the dwarf than to the giant.

My first story was about a giant because the first thing I read and fell in love with was about a giant. I was seven when I read that Oscar Wilde story. Some children play in the giant's garden. Time passes, and eventually the giant gets old and frail and can't play with the children any more. He sits in a giant armchair, watching them play, admiring his garden, looking around him. I was a big fan of Oscar Wilde's giant, so I put the giant in my version on the patio behind my house. My parents and the neighbours got on well with him too, so he grew old out there on the patio. Sometimes the giant went with me to the market.

A giant armchair. The dwarf's made-to-measure furniture. The medium-sized wooden chair I'm sitting on. The giant who plays games, the dwarf with his elegant cane. What's the median? Is the average a point in between the two ends? Is there an exact centre? Is the present a kind of average? Am I all the sizes of handwriting I've ever had? Do my handwriting and its diminutive size contain my big writing from when I was a child?

Does this story contain all the stories I am?

It's Sunday. I'm going to the cinema with Guillermo. But before I leave I'm going to tell you something, Jonás. I love you, I miss you so much.

Emmanuel Bove's first novel is called *My Friends*. It was published in 1924, when Bove was twenty-six. I've been looking for this book for years. To no avail. The only part of the book I've read is the title. I think it's beautiful because it's so simple. If I weren't going to the cinema tonight, I'd write a version of *My Friends*. Tania, Carolina, Julia, Guillermo, Tepepunk, Antonio and Luis Felipe would be the seven chapters of that novel I'm not going to write. Jonás would feature in all of them.

I'm back from the cinema. Part of the magic of the ideal notebook is that hours, days and weeks can go by from one paragraph to the next, but because the paragraphs live side by side like neighbours, it's as if only a few minutes have passed. Amazing – something that takes years to write could be read by someone else in a couple of hours.

The dwarf, Jonás and I form this story, but we could also form a band. Music for two identical notebooks and a piccolo cane.

On the way back from the cinema, Guillermo pointed out an advert in the street. 'Do you want to grow taller?' it said, beneath a photo of some platform shoes. I asked him to drive more slowly so I could read the small print. He said that when he was a teenager his mother took him to a growth clinic. The doctor told her he was the height of a Lacandon Indian. His mother was worried, she wanted her son to be taller. Guillermo refused to go ahead with the procedure: 'We're the same height, mum, what are you talking about?' His mother bought him some platform shoes. 'Mum, please!' said Guillermo when he opened the box.

I haven't mentioned this, Jonás, but if you were here, I can assure you I wouldn't be writing.

A question. While she was waiting, did Penelope masturbate?

Do you think this trip is pushing us apart or bringing us together? I've also set off on a journey. This journey. Twenty thousand leagues under the notebook. A journey with no destination. An infinite queue. An eternal waiting room. I don't really know how it will end. I don't know where I'll end up. Or if I'll end up anywhere. Where am I going?

Now that I'm phosphorescent I can see Jonás in a bedroom in one of his aunts' houses in Valencia. In my phosphorescent state I can see Julia smoking before she goes to sleep, and Carolina lying on one side, her belly large, and Tania getting an early night, because she said she was jetlagged today after coming back from her exhibition in Basel. In my phosphorescence I fly over all the people I love, and my light goes out when I get into bed.

Last night I wrote Jonás a long email. Now I don't feel like writing or talking.

My notebook is my guitar. I miss Jonás so much. And what if everything's over when he comes back? I'm scared, I don't want it to end, it feels strange that he's not here. Every love song sounds the same and it's Orpheus' fault. The Greek curse has hit all the radio stations.

Tragedy is a change of scale. Jonás' mum died tragically. Jonás' tragedy seems to give him a different scale to other people. He feels misunderstood. Feeling misunderstood seems to make him a different size. Perhaps that's why he's isolating himself, why he's running away. But what is there to run away from if we can't run away from ourselves?

A garden full of trees: that was the *locus amoenus* in medieval times. My *locus amoenus* is this notebook. It's where I play the guitar. Where I feel sad. Where I'm horribly sentimental. Oh, my little notebook that was a bush in a past life.

Wind is easily dealt with. You can close a window, zip up a sweater. But the sea is invincible. In that sense, Poseidon is a fiction. That's why I find him the most beguiling of all the Greek gods. In *The Iliad* they give him the sea. Here you go, it's all yours. The waves of the sea: the blue lines in your notebook. With a favourable wind, perhaps these lines will carry you to shore.

A fork is Poseidon's dwarf trident. You can stir up the waters in this glass to prove it.

If beautiful Helen of Troy had had an aquiline nose, the course of History would have been different. If I'd bought vanilla ice cream instead of mango sorbet, perhaps we wouldn't have moved in together so soon after meeting. How can we know? The slightest thing can change the course of any story.

I'm not sad any more. One advantage of being born under the sign of Wild is the Wind is that you can move easily from place to place, like the woman with blue eyeliner told me.

Change. Unlearning yourself is more important than knowing yourself.

Today I saw a dwarf in the distance and thought it was the dwarf from my block, but it wasn't. This one didn't smile at me.

I bought some biscuits that were really delicious, but a bit expensive. I recommended them to Tania. Before I'd finished describing them, she cut me off: 'Listen, I used to buy Barilla spaghetti. I'd spend fifteen pesos and make pasta that kept for three days in the fridge. Ever since I discovered this fancy Italian brand I've been spending a hundred pesos on some fusilli that only lasts one sitting. It's hopeless, I can't go back to Barilla now. That's the thing, you can never go back. Maybe it's the curse of nice things. The other day a collector's secretary offered me a coffee, rubbing her hands like she was trying to tempt me. And it was instant! I'm sorry, but once you taste good coffee you can't go back. Forget it. It's like good sex, once you discover it, there's no going back. So forget it, I'm not trying these biscuits you're talking about. I'm sure they're better than my María biscuits. But seriously, forget it.'

No news from Jonás.

Tepepunk and Nina arrived at their residency in Tokyo a few days ago. This is how Tepepunk's email begins: 'I'm writing to you from the future, and from here I can tell you that everything's going to be OK with Jonás. I should also tell you that in the future I have very precise dreams and every afternoon I drink tea with a wise Japanese man. Now's your chance: I'm in the future, ask me anything you like. I'm your oracle.'

The cat trapped his paw in an armchair. He got hurt, I took him to the vet. Luckily it wasn't serious. Back home, I called Tania. 'I've realised I really love the cat,' I told her. 'I love him too much.' 'I need a pet,' she said, 'but I'm allergic to cats. Maybe a dog? No. They need a lot of attention, you can't have two needy personalities like that under one roof. A fish? No, I don't like them, they don't do anything. Remember how there used to be fish tanks everywhere in the eighties? Hilarious. Even on the ceilings. A ferret? No way, not even a juggling one. They're basically sausage-rats. I know, I'll buy a canary. A canary in a cage. Do you know if you can get plastic canaries?'

A long day of work and endless admin. I arrive home wanting to write the opera *Bureaucracy* in three acts. The main character would deliver an intense soliloquy in front of the photocopier. I imagine this main character, an office-worker. There's a beautiful woman, coveted by everyone in the office. The main character would compete, he'd fight for her love. He wouldn't manage to win her, and the situation would spiral out of control. An apocalyptic moment: the lights in the office begin to fail, some of the bulbs blow. Photocopies whirl around in the air. The telephones all ring at once, the computers turn off and on. The fluffy animals, picture frames and miniature toys on the monitors bounce up and down, and some tumble to the floor. A fax machine goes crazy, the photocopier hurls itself against the window. It's time for the main character's anagnorisis: he sings.

Opera, musicals. Two genres I don't like. Still, as soon as I work out whether I'm getting closer or getting further away I think I'll burst into song.

This evening I went for a walk in the park. Near the paved area, I saw two girls holding hands. Two sisters in different school uniforms. When I passed close to them, I realised one was blind. The younger girl, who was around seven, was leading her by the hand and describing what she saw, the trees, the dried-up fountain, a dog running along. 'And what do you think the doggie's called?' her older sister asked. 'Oh, he's called Doggie, of course,' the younger girl answered. A girl who sees the world through what her younger sister tells her. This is love, I thought, pure and simple. Isn't the voice, at the end of the day, made for other people to hear it? And aren't stories what create bonds? Isn't trying to describe what the other person can't see an act of love?

9

I'm in the waiting area. They've just announced that the flight's delayed. This situation is also the shortest possible summary of this story.

I'm at the airport. A man in a fluorescent yellow jacket is pushing a miniscule old lady in a wheelchair. The old lady, like the Sibyl in the *Metamorphoses*, is shrinking by the day. Or so it seems. I'd say she's probably the same height standing up as she is sitting down. In this waiting area, at the back, there's a Mennonite couple. They're dressed in sombre colours. It's like fluorescent yellow is a technological advance they'll arrive at in a few centuries' time, if at all.

Perhaps if an old lady lived for enough decades she'd end up the same height as a dwarf.

I find the following products in the in-flight magazine: 'Bigfoot, the ideal garden statue' and 'Gnomes, an ideal set of statues for the home'. '

I'm fascinated by anything useless. The more useless an object, the more of a triumph I think it is. As if it were made more to tell a story than to be of use to anyone. I'm the kind of person who'll buy a drink because they like the look of the bottle. Even if I don't like the drink,

I'll appreciate the bottle. In other words, I'd sooner buy a kaleidoscope than a vacuum cleaner. I wouldn't buy the resin gnomes because I don't like them, but I imagine the shrinking old lady might have Bigfoot in her garden. On her behalf, I ask something that perhaps she'd also like to know: why is Bigfoot not ideal for interiors?

I imagine the conversation between the Mennonites flicking through the airline's magazine of useless products.

A hologram of Clarice Lispector appears in the seat next to me: 'I should have liked to be other people first in order to know what I was not. Then I realised that I had already been those others and found it easy. My greatest experience would be to be the other of the others: and the other of the others was me.'

In a gossip magazine I see that the Most Important Artist in Mexico is having a retrospective at the Tate Modern. I like his work, I find some of his pieces interesting; I think they're good, they have depth. But fame doesn't care about the work. In the article he's standing between two tall, toned, glamorous women. There's a picture of the gallery on one side, but not a single photo of his work. This cult of importance has strange ideas about what's important.

It would be ideal if Jonás were sitting next to me, on this plane heading for Chicago. He might go on a rant about the gossip magazine. But I enjoy visiting the outskirts like this, not to mention they have the best horoscopes.

Last night, before setting off, I spoke to Antonio: pure gossip, tabloid gossip about everyone we know. My friendship with Antonio is based on occasional phonecalls, long conversations in amongst the emails and texts. He lives abroad, with his wife and two daughters. Talking to him is a lot of fun. Our conversations are a closed circuit of in-jokes and nicknames – everyone has a nickname, we stopped calling people by their names and surnames long ago. I feel like whenever I see my friend Antonio's name flash up, no one will get out alive.

I'm in Chicago. Since the event organiser didn't have much money, she said I could stay with one of her friends. I'm in the home of a girl who's away on a trip; I don't know her, but I like her based on her apartment. If this apartment were an object, it would be a hand-knitted blanket. She seems like a sentimental girl. Sweet, kind-hearted. There's a lot of colour here. She has family photos, plastic figurines in the plant pots, plants. And a Shakespeare quote on a fridge magnet: 'A hundred thousand welcomes! I could weep, / And I could laugh; I am light and heavy. Welcome!'

If someone asked me for a full-length portrait of myself, I'd show them that Shakespeare quote. Why does a girl I don't know, who's let me stay in her apartment for a few days, have that quote on her fridge? Maybe if we went into strangers' houses and snooped around in the drawers we'd be surprised by how much we have in common.

I'm in the kitchen. I can hear the hum of the fridge and the water dripping in the sink. They're familiar sounds, a strange way of feeling at home even when you're in the home of a total stranger. In this kitchen there are two Mexican *lotería* boards in frames, with the usual pictures instead of numbers. I see there's no dwarf among the images, no sea or notebook, but there is a bird. The lady and the hand are next to each other. If I had to sum up the history of the world for an alien I'd use those two images from the Mexican *lotería*: the lady and the hand. A good synthesis, from Helen of Troy to the woman walking into a 7-Eleven; and the hand which destroyed and built everything, including that 7-Eleven.

I flick through a magazine in the bathroom. I half-read an article: 'The carpet mafia in Pakistan'. There are no photos. I imagine the leader of the carpet mafia. If I could form a mafia, I'd form the useless things mafia. It would be a mafia with no power. We'd traffic in the best kaleidoscopes on the market.

Halloween is a good time of year in the States. Fancy dress, parties all over the place. I could seize my chance and dress up as a swallow. Or dress up as Proust in order to turn into a swallow halfway through a conversation. Let go of my beer, just like that, and start flapping my wings in the middle of the party. Fly out through the window.

I know that the mother of the girl whose apartment I'm staying in died, and I know she's now at her father's wedding to another woman. A very young woman, the same age as the daughter, the event organiser told me. Meanwhile, Jonás, Marina and their father are travelling around Spain. I don't think Jonás' father will marry again. It doesn't seem to matter to him that he could. When he talks about his wife, it sounds like she was the first, and will be the last and only, woman in his life.

Looking closely at someone else's apartment is a way of putting on someone else's shoes. Here you can feel the loss in every corner. She lives alone. There's a magnet from a hospital on the fridge, and photos of her mother at different ages in the living room. In the bedroom there's an affectionate message of condolence, tacked to a noticeboard with colourful pins. Next to the wardrobe there's a little black-and-white photo of her mother. Jonás has a photo of his mother in the study we share. A big photo, in black and white, of his mother as a young woman in the seventies, when she was studying chemistry at university. Jonás wanted to put it in the bedroom, and I suggested putting it in the study. 'Help me choose a place for it in the study,' Jonás said. Now I wonder if we should have put the photo of his mother in the bedroom.

Suddenly I'm afraid of my mother dying. It's a fear I've had on and off since I was a girl. It doesn't change, it feels the same as it did when I was seven. Nevertheless, when I turned thirty it settled in a different place. Last year, when the two nurses opened the door to the room and the first thing I saw was the relief on my mother's face, I realised the story had to be the other way around. In other words, the story goes like this: a child doesn't want to cause their parents that amount of pain. When the time comes, the child has to bury the parents, not the other way round. It's the desirable order.

How similar are the desirable and the ideal?

In the first nightmares I can remember, my mother would disappear. Meanwhile, it wasn't in dreams that my father disappeared. He spent most of his time at work and was hardly ever at home, and as a result his absences felt normal. My mother's absences meant something else. In the nightmares, I'd be following my mother's voice – running through a forest, down endless staircases, searching a square; I followed her voice, but it grew fainter and fainter until I could no longer hear it. Shouting for my mother woke me up more than once. I'd go and peer round the door to my parents' bedroom to make sure she was still there. If she wasn't, I'd ask my father questions until he managed to calm me down. As well as a favourite bird, the other thing I share with Proust is this dependence on our mothers. Mothers equally loving, pretty, quick-witted. I think I've just made my Proust costume.

The day after the accident – that is, when I'd opened my eyes and was beginning the recovery process – my mother had a diabetic attack. Like when a burnt-out office-worker succumbs to the flu as soon as his holidays begin. My father came in to reassure me: 'The doctor says it's normal, it was the shock, but it's not serious, darling. She'll stabilise again soon, you'll see.'

So the journey to the bottom of the notebook is also the journey to the bottom of loss. Being here makes me see Jonás' loss differently. Being in this apartment has changed my point of view, as if I'd shifted a few centimetres to look at Jonás' loss from another angle. The third person is sometimes a place you have to travel to.

My mum took ballet classes as a girl. She was skinny, with freckles on her face and shoulders and she wore a pink tutu. I have that photo in the study, near the photo of Jonás' mother. When Jonás tells me something about Ana, or when his father or Marina have told me things about her, that's the image in my head. I've seen other photos, but that's the image I see every day and the one I usually multiply and animate, as if I'm making a film and it doesn't matter when the action takes place: Ana is always twenty-three and a smiling university student. My mother looks nothing like the girl in the pink tutu. She has a strong character, she's proud of her grey hair and her age, she has a keen intuition and a good sense of humour. As if the Spanish frankness and Portuguese melancholy had been added together, rather than subtracted to leave the pessimism they sometimes leave. I think Jonás' mother and mine would have got along well. I imagine them drinking coffee together in the kitchen at home. In our apartment, I mean.

You have to travel a long way to get close to the person you sleep beside. And perhaps I've also had to travel this far to get close to myself.

'I dreamed about my mum, love, a weird dream that's been in my head all day. I'll call you later,' the text message from Jonás said.

Last night, on the way out of a bar, a stranger gave me two lollies. The only idea I've had all day is that the zombie lollies – heads made of toffee – should have bubble-gum brains. Then you'd feel like a zombie eating the zombie lolly. A meta-zombie.

My friend Luis Felipe wrote a poem about zombies, which alluded to the obscene number of violent deaths in Mexico. I'm going to keep a lolly for him, like a souvenir of his own poem.

I see a framed photo in this café and wonder if the person in it is dead or alive. The uncertainty of framed photos. Frames are like names: the people they contain might be dead or alive, but at that precise moment they're in the photo, in that gerund. That name which goes on, that continuous present, that frame, those static letters forming our name. Disconcertingly immortal.

Yesterday evening I bought some records. Not a very common practice these days. You might even call it eccentric. Hardly anyone buys records. I know they're clumsy and not very practical, and that nowadays music is free. But I like buying records. One of the ones I bought was *Station to Station* by David Bowie, which includes 'Wild is the Wind'.

In Search of Lost Time. When I buy records, when I watch the laundry spinning in the machine, when I spend ages in the shower, when I go the long way home from work, when I watch the cat sleeping, when I deliberately waste time on the computer, I feel like Proust's title is a miniscule monument.

In this café, to my right, there's a brass globe. An antique. I look at the distance between the United States, Spain and Mexico and see a lopsided triangle. Jonás, the black cat in the apartment and me.

Drinking beer in the kitchen last night with people from the event, something reminded me of when we used to live in the States. My parents unpacking boxes, talking in the kitchen, smoking and drinking beer with the neighbours while my brother and I chatted in the garden. Something about that instant familiarity. But this time I felt further away. I know it's a simple observation, but the electric pencil sharpener – that distance I thought I could see between adult life and childhood – seems like a recent invention, something I wrote about not long ago. As if that whole time we spent living in San Francisco, that night I remember when the neighbours came round, were also things I'd invented. Childhood is so uncertain, so distant. It's almost like childhood is the origin of fiction: describing any past event over and over to see how far away you're getting from reality.

I've been invited to a party. I don't know whether to stay in and read instead. I like what I'm reading so much that if Proust were a madeleine I'd dress as a cup of tea. In fact, if Proust were alive and in Chicago, I'd invite him to the party. I bet it would be fun to go to a party with Proust. He'd be the first on the dancefloor.

I expect my Proust looks more like a piñata by now than like someone who really existed. Words carry us far away, always so far away from reality.

At the party I told one of the guests about my ideal notebook. 'What do you mean?' she asked. 'Nothing happens? A waiting room?' What she didn't say: the work in progress, the story with no beginning or end, useless things. Studying communication, buying books and records. Watching films. Going to La Lagunilla to browse the second-hand furniture, going to a flea market, a garage sale. Buying a vase and some artificial flowers. Buying an ashtray to keep the house keys in. Making things useless. Taking the hands off the watch, wearing it as a bracelet to make it useless. Writing, reading. I've done all these things. This is more or less how I spend my days.

Am I getting closer or am I getting further away?

Oh, I have so many questions. All unusable. I prefer questions to answers. Being on the way is better, you can open the windows and let the wind mess up your hair. I love messing up my hair. I could hold a garage sale with all the questions I've accumulated here – I have so many, piled up like pieces of junk. I also have freezing hands. I'm in a park. It's cold and very windy.

Yesterday the organiser held a goodbye party. We stayed up drinking until late. I had the Bowie record I'd bought in my rucksack. It was a nice surprise to find that the guests knew 'Wild is the Wind' so well, and we even sang it all together. An excellent goodbye party. I remembered the musical, *Chicago*. Wild is the Windy City.

At the American Airlines counter, I was served by a woman of around sixty who was dressed as a witch. 'Where's your broom?' I asked her. 'Oh, we modern witches travel by Thunderbird. The next time you see a Thunderbird, watch out: there'll be a witch like me inside it,' she said, handing back my passport.

On the plane, I catch a potent whiff of BO from the woman two seats away. I wish I could open the window. We've just gone through some turbulence. The pilot's turning circles, or so it seems. Sharp bends and turbulence, what terror is made of. I remember that Bolaño character, the pilot who writes poems in the air.

Stopover in Dallas. At the airline counter, I got the costume of the man who served me wrong. I thought he was a black rabbit, but actually he was a bat. A man of fifty, I'd guess. 'Let me show you what I really am,' he said, stepping out from behind the counter and stretching his arms to display his purple satin wings. He flapped them a few times.

Now I'm going to write something important: bats have smaller ears than rabbits. And Halloween allows the United States a childlike breathing space, a playful interlude. I wouldn't be surprised to see the president of the United States dressed as a pumpkin in the middle of a government meeting.

In Mexico, despite La Catrina and sugar skulls, death is a sensitive subject. The facts mean we can't be flippant about it. If the Mexican president put on a fancy-dress costume, for example, he'd be dragged out of his office feet first.

I don't understand people who are scared of flying. The plane's instability is what appeals to me. I don't mean the turbulence; I mean the act of flying along calmly, thinking that if everything has to end, you could be in the air, in a cinema or lying in bed. Lying in bed, which is where I was just before I learnt that the accident had caused the problem with my gallbladder, a kind of domino effect. And now I think it's a good thing I went through that, because to travel more lightly, to lose your fear, you don't even need to leave the house. Afraid of what, why or to what end? From one moment to the next everything can change. You have to relax when travelling by plane, vulnerability is everywhere because the vulnerability is us. Plus it's nice to see the clouds from above. Oh, that false omniscience. What I really love is seeing the clouds move. A film of moving clouds is a good way to waste time. And it's even better if I listen to José José singing: 'Even the swallow emigrated, foreseeing the end.'

10

Jonás has decided to postpone his return. His plan is to go to Trévago and then visit a couple of friends in Paris who've just had a baby, since Marcos can stand in for him at work. His father and sister came back on Friday. Marina called to say that Jonás sent a few things for me, and that I can go over for dinner whenever I want. 'My dad and I brought you something, too,' she said.

Tania on the phone: 'How do people unwind? For example, people who don't read think reading is unwinding. But if you read, drink coffee and pace around your office and that's part of your job, how do you unwind at the weekend? Pace around your apartment in slippers until it's Monday again? No, my dear: that's work!'

Someone in the office read me a news article and suddenly writing seemed like making a watery soup. And I don't like watery soup. Perhaps this, an anecdote I like from John Cage, will give the soup some flavour: 'One evening when I was still living at Grand Street and Monroe, Isamu Noguchi came to visit me. There was nothing in the room (no furniture, no paintings). The floor was covered, wall to wall, with cocoa matting. The windows had no curtains, no drapes. Isamu Noguchi said, "An old shoe would look beautiful in this room."'

Maybe one of your shoes, in the middle of this blank page, would look beautiful.

It's Sunday. I like Sunday nights, and this particular time always puts me in a good mood. It's the National Hour on the radio. The airport hour, Sunday from ten to eleven p.m. A transition into Monday, a waiting room. Normally, when Jonás is here, at this time we're watching a film, having dinner or driving home in the car.

Today I was wondering what my metamorphosis would be. What my true metamorphosis would be, I mean, if such a thing were possible. I'd like to turn into a swallow, I know that, but I wondered what I'd really turn into. What if I became a duck or a rock?

Daphne, for example, turned into a tree. Her metamorphosis wasn't a punishment. She wanted it so much and so deeply that in the end it happened. Her words granted her the transformation. Metamorphosis is the continuation of a character's story: it can be a punishment or a gift. I wonder if the written word has the same power, if words can change us like that. If writing and reading transform us into something we have yet to discover.

During the weeks I spent recovering in hospital, and then in the apartment where I lived briefly before moving in with Jonás, I remember it was raining. Hours, days, weeks of rain. I watched it fall. First lying down, then sitting up. Anyone who's been in that kind of situation knows how the physical pain presses you up close against the present. This hurts, that's injured, I'm cold, I'm hungry, I need the bathroom, I'm falling asleep, are the kinds of thoughts that subject each moment, each second, to being there. There in the present, which lasts longer the more painful it is. When the recovery begins, when you're gradually getting better, there's a window, a small frame through which you can project yourself into another time – into the future. In spite of the rain, during that period I thought about what I wanted to do when the sun came out. At the end of the day, that's what low points are for: to open that window. I thought a lot about doing everything I'd been too afraid to do, and that was the window I had. When I met Jonás I flung myself through it, with all my weight.

11

This afternoon I heard a man in an ice-cream parlour say to his wife: 'We can leave the dwarves with your mother, darling.' It struck me as a sentence with cruelty at its core. Children as dwarves, dwarves as children. Evidently a question of height.

I haven't seen the dwarf on the block for a while. I wonder what he'd turn into. Perhaps a lynx. If the cat turned into a person I think he'd like to be my boyfriend. He'd be jealous, unreasonable. Right now he's lying on top of me, with two paws in my lap and the other two on my shoulder. His eyes are closed and he's purring. It even seems like he cares about me.

I dreamed about Ernesto, my ex-boyfriend, and his dad. The three of us were in a restaurant, having lunch with a strange character. This person wasn't very entertaining, but he was making all kinds of efforts to win our favour; an unpleasant, obnoxious man, all in all. Ernesto's father, through facial expressions, gestures, movements and comments, delicately shielded us from him. Ernesto got up suddenly to go to the toilet and didn't come back. I felt comfortable and protected by his father. Just like when he was alive, I thought when I woke up.

Dreaming about Ernesto's father, whom I loved so much, made me feel strangely looked-after.

Julia gave me a book about small, almost imperceptible islands. It reminded me of my dear, elegant friend on the block. The first island in the book:

Lonely Island (Russia)
Russian Ostrov Uyedineniya 'Solitude Island'
20 km² | uninhabited
Loneliness lies in the centre of the Kara Sea in the northern Arctic Ocean.

An island has another scale, other rules of growth; the sea decides the pattern of an island's development. The island that's twenty kilometres from end to end, and is called Lonely Island, carries the tautology in its name.

An island is like someone who's deaf. A space with which communication is difficult. Being deaf, unable to hear, is a way of being an island. And in that way, like an isolated phrase, badly communicated, not listening to the others, I'll say that I don't know the whole of the national anthem but I know entire Juan Gabriel songs off by heart. '*Siempre en mi mente*' could be the anthem for this apartment. Always on my mind.

To write is to maroon yourself on an island the size of a page.

I thought about the famous hypothetical game about the island. The ideal island to which you can take books, records, friends, as an exercise in choice.

When I was a teenager, my father helped me change the toner cartridge in the printer. He did a test. Thinking he should write something to try out the printer belonging to his daughter, who was studying communication at university, who liked reading, my father wrote the first thing that came into his head, in the middle of a blank sheet of paper: 'A word all alone'. But that word isn't alone, dad. And what's more, that line you wrote is a good snapshot of you. You're never alone. And yet.

My father's handwriting is difficult to read, difficult to understand. He has trouble communicating. I could never copy his signature at secondary school. It's like a closed circuit. A kind of island handwriting?

The word loneliness is unlikely to be alone. In the name Lonely Island it naturally forms an adjective, a fitting one for any isolation.

I'm on a plane to the Oaxaca Book Fair. At the airport, I bought a guide to the common birds of Mexico City. According to that guide there are two common kinds of swallow. One, the barn swallow (*cuicuitzcatl*, in Nahuatl), has a black mask, a red face and a yellow body. A subdued yellow, like the body of my Bic pen, which, by the way, has a black lid. The covers of my notebook are red. When I write in this notebook and leave my Bic pen between the pages, it makes the three colours of the common swallow of Mexico City. If my notebook began whistling a Juan Gabriel song, it would be my ideal notebook.

I've got the guitar. My notebook is my guitar, though it's not always in tune. Maybe when I reach the hotel I can write a song about how similar birds are to open books.

I'm eating a delicious plate of chicken with *mole* sauce and handmade blue tortillas. I think Oaxacan food deserves its own small island, with a national anthem and flag.

The stationer's in Oaxaca where I bought my Ideal notebooks today is called El Águila. The Eagle. It's on Calle Morelos and there's a lovely little old lady behind the counter who's had the shop for sixty years. Her daughter was there, too. An attentive woman in her early forties, with a crucifix hanging from a thin gold chain. I started talking to her. She patiently showed me various notebooks, and although I didn't find one identical to mine – the *cuicuitzcatl* – I bought four with black covers, in different sizes. Since they didn't have the kind I was looking for, we ended up having a discussion about notebooks. The old lady got involved: 'These notebooks are all very good quality, you see. They're hand-sewn, the way people used to make them in my day. That's why I buy them. But there was a time, miss, when I couldn't get hold of them: the owners died and the kids didn't keep the business going. Up in Mexico State, that's where the family are with their bookbinding workshop. Now the grandchildren have taken it up again and I put in an order every six months. But they're not like other brands, ones with big factories that can handle all the orders from offices and schools and what have you. No, miss, not at all. For instance, a fellow who works in the council came in here wanting some leather folders, the kind I get from a man who lives in the Isthmus, up in the hills. He was after a hundred folders to give to his whole office at Christmas. And, well, that's not how it works, is it? I've got five folders because they're the five folders the man can make: he makes them by hand. You see what I mean, people think you can get hold of anything just like that, that everything's done on modern machines,

78

that people make lots of the same thing, but there are still little family-run bookbinding workshops or people who make five folders in half a year. But the Ideal notebooks aren't like the big notebook factories. That's why I don't have the red notebooks you're after, miss, now I only have the black ones. Like I say, I couldn't get hold of any for a while, and it took me years to get back in touch through the grandchildren; the children wanted nothing to do with it. Who knows what the children are up to and why they aren't keen on their father's bookbinding business – and him such a kind, hard-working man. But the grandchildren took it up again. Honestly, that makes me think maybe my grandchildren love me more than my children do. But then, you never know. Still, that's the thing: grandchildren are like that, they're easier to mould, they stay closer to you, they love you more, isn't that right? And they're the ones who keep making the notebooks like they made them in my day: top-quality. Look, they're sewn, the edges are tinted with red, the pages are nice and thick. You could write in fountain pen without it going through to the other side. But people nowadays don't think about that stuff. They don't look at what they buy. Isn't it true, miss, that the Ideal notebooks are very good? Now, listen, every year I get Christmas presents made for my lifelong clients. Do you smoke? Not any more? I've never smoked, but so you can put some sweets in your living room I'm going to give you this black pottery ashtray I had made with the name of my shop on it. Just a moment. Here you go, isn't it lovely? Made here in Oaxaca. It's for you.'

At breakfast Luis Felipe told me there's a poet who calls his wife 'beloved'. 'How do you mean?' I asked. 'Just like that. In public, wherever, he'll say: "Beloved, could you pass the sugar?" Or: "Beloved, the bread, please."'

Luis Felipe smokes a lot. Tonight we were drinking mezcal, he lit a cigarette and I felt like smoking too. I used to smoke a lot before the accident. Loads. I started when I was at university. At first I didn't smoke much, one or two a day. After the accident – before I hallucinated that the blanket covering me was an exotic plant with a temperature of forty degrees – and my gallbladder ruptured, that day I smoked a whole packet and had to go back to hospital. Like almost all the days leading up to that, I was smoking Marlboros. I have a sudden urge to smoke now. I decided to give up because it seemed like my activities had become nothing more than a thread which, like the thread in a necklace, connected my twenty a day. It's so important to be able to see yourself differently, although when I'm with my friend and he's smoking and the conversation's really flowing, it makes me want to go back to it. Maybe I could start again, but only when I'm chatting to Luis Felipe.

Missed call from Jonás. I'll try calling back.

Last night I heard a bad poet read. As I listened to the soporific verses dedicated to his beloved, I felt like I was watching a snail glide from one side of a floor tile to the other. His words were like a long trail of slime.

There's a church in Oaxaca with a statue in it called Holy Child, Mover of Hearts. The sheer quantity of balloons, cards, votive offerings and candles beneath it is enough to move the heart. If I hadn't been with my friend, I would have knelt down and begged for Jonás to come back.

I remembered the Holy Child of Grants. He could have a place in a church somewhere. The Divine Child who holds a scroll in his left hand, a piece of parchment showing the terms and conditions of the grant. The Holy Child has a miniature chair. I could offer the service of dressing the Saint. Provide accessories like a basket, carrycot or cradle. A stand to prop the Divine Child upright. A bell jar, glass case or cabinet to display him in if you're awarded the grant. Flowers, electric candles, literary medals, stamps, lithographs, miniature books of poems, state prizes, vinyl records, scale models. Or any other item produced by Mexican artists between the ages of eighteen and thirty-five who want to be considered for the grant.

The altar and the work dedicated to the Divine Child. So many books. Short films, full-length films, theatre productions. In his colourful corner of the church there are balloons, letters, artworks, records, poetry pamphlets, photos from Young Creators' events, passport-size photos of grateful Young Creators. Rumour has it that, among the offerings to the Child, there are purple velvet pouches containing marijuana and other drugs.

I'm back from Oaxaca. Today I had to make a lot of phone calls for work. I've used up my daily quota of words. All I achieved was drawing a spiral on the back of a receipt while on the phone to someone, I forget who. Our Lady of Silence covers me tonight with her white veil.

Jonás says he'd like to come home soon, that he misses me. I don't know what to tell him. Here I am. I suddenly wonder: what will he be like when he comes back? Has anything about him changed? Is he still looking for something connected to his mother that he hasn't found? Will he ever find it? That's why his journey is so long: he can't find peace. And what if he returns only to come face-to-face with the despair that made him set off in the first place? His life is on pause. The loss, the farewell, the death of his mother, are its themes. Indirectly, too: everything he does, everything he's now afraid of, relates to the same things. What can I do? Nothing, of course. But I like to think I could do something for him. Believe in him, be with him, keep him company. I'd like to give him what he needs, in the way he needs it. So here I am.

Sometimes I'm afraid. I wonder what will happen when Jonás returns from his trip. Sometimes I worry that when he comes back this will all be over, but then, I'm scared of endings in general. It's a consequence of the accident. Sometimes I'm scared of the end of the day, and sometimes I think that when he gets back from his trip a new, positive phase of our relationship will begin. Still, here I am. I flung myself through the window with all my weight and now there's no going back. Like in 'Wild is the Wind', I'll go anywhere with you.

I'd like to be a swallow so I could visit the dwarf, so I could chat to him. I'd like to be able to knock on the front door of that man I find so intriguing, have a few drinks, talk and talk without looking at the time. I'm sure we'd have a lot to say to each other. What would the dwarf think of my waiting?

A swallow's nest is shaped like a cup, I read on the internet. I go and get my cup of coffee so I can carry on reading: 'The swallow's song is a cheerful warble which often ends in a *su-seer*, with the second note higher than the first. The calls include a *witt* or a *witt-witt*, or a loud *splee-plink* when they're overexcited or when they attempt to scare predators away from the area around their nests.'

When Jonás comes back, I don't know if he'll sing a

witt-witt or a loud *splee-plink*. It depends how threatened he thinks the nest is. And that's the thing: for now, as Jonás sees it, the nest is with his mother. Or with the idea of his mother. Not here, with me, in this apartment which is also his. That's why he's away.

It continues: 'The common swallow was described by Carl Linnaeus in 1758 in the tenth edition of his work *Systema Naturae* using the scientific name of *Hirundo rustica. Hirundo* means swallow in Latin; *rusticus*, from the countryside.' I love you, Jonás. I'm rustic. The swallow is a small bird, and migratory. If you want to stay in Spain, I can go there. If you want us to be apart for a while, that's fine too.

I read that swallows sing individually and in unison. Common swallows generally reproduce between May and August, but we can make an exception now it's December, Jonás. And look at this: 'Reproductive success is related to the length of the male bird's tail.' I'm telling a long tale for you now, Jonás.

'The swallow symbolises the coming of spring and love in *Pervigilium Veneris*.' Oh, I just love Wikipedia. Such a shame I had to study in the library when I was a student, surrounded by photocopies and books, index cards and highlighters. The kind of information I like is right here, in every colour at once. The internet is like a chewing-gum machine and a blue piece has just popped out, my favourite colour: 'The common swallow is the national bird of Estonia.'

If this apartment we live in is the size of a small island, we could have a regional bird. I read that swallows are a symbol of loyalty, that they choose a partner for life.

12

A long phone conversation with Jonás. It's Friday night, my slippers are on and I've just watered the plants. I'm curled up in the armchair. The cat's curled up here too, purring, like a miniature soul in slippers as well. Oh, I love spending Friday nights like this so much. I'd put some music on, but the cat's just dozed off. I don't dare wake him. A sleeping cat, that domestic dictatorship.

I wonder if Jonás has slept with anyone. Is a French girl removing her hairband even as I write and placing it by Jonás' watch? Or is a Spanish girl sitting in bed beside him, lighting a post-coital cigarette? I'd better stop, this is making me horribly anxious. I like questions, but not all of them.

The old watch, the wind-up watch his father gave him. The watch that belonged to his grandfather, his father's father. Jonás takes it off every night before going to sleep. I miss the presence of that watch on the nightstand.

I saw Carolina, whose belly is getting bigger and bigger. Julia called from Canada, she's at a film festival. She's happy because she bought a new guitar after a meeting. Tania called to say that books with tiny print make her feel like she's on a treadmill, wearing jogging bottoms, and getting nowhere. 'It's awful, you just don't move.'

Julia said she desperately needed to come home, to have a drink and a chat. Carolina said Lila was very fidgety this afternoon, but I didn't get to feel her kicking.

I had lunch with Philippe and Luis Felipe. I realised Philippe is responsible for Vila-Matas encountering Emmanuel Bove. This means he's also responsible for my spending all this time hunting for a copy of *My Friends*, which Vila-Matas mentions in his book dedicated to Robert Walser, one of my favourite writers. Oh, it's wonderful when one book leads you to another. A novel I've been trying to track down for ages, like a kind of savage detective. In the university library there was a copy of another book by Bove. 'It's his last novel, but I prefer *Mes amis*, the first one,' said Philippe. I have Bove's last novel photocopied on my bookshelf, a kind of adopted sibling to its out-of-print brothers and sisters.

If I wrote about my friends, I'd dedicate chapters to Tania, Julia, Carolina, Guillermo, Tepepunk, Antonio and Luis Felipe. Jonás would appear too. I'd like to write a novel called *My Friends*. The chapter about Luis Felipe could be a long sentimental conversation over mezcal and cigarettes, and include the self-help verses and passages that come up as we talk. The chapter could end in a karaoke bar in the early hours, the two of us singing pop songs with our arms around each other. For the chapter about Tepepunk, I'd choose five or six emails in which he describes his days in Tokyo, the city as he discovers it with Nina. The constant comparisons with Mexico City from his point-of-view. I'd alternate the texts with the photos he sends of their walks. I could include the one he sent me recently, accompanied by this note: 'Can you believe I stole these 3D glasses from a museum without realising? I walked out with them on, just like that, casual as anything.' For Guillermo's chapter I could choose a long night in a cantina, his sense of humour a magnet attracting stories like iron filings. Our long conversation would end just before sunrise; we'd be walking through a park, Guillermo would stop and chat to a street-sweeper, and at the end of the chapter he'd give the street-sweeper a hug. I think Antonio's daughters would provide a good portrait of their father, so his chapter could be a dialogue between them. The novel about my friends would be like a love letter. I'd make a character sketch of each of them. Come to think of it, I don't know how I'd talk about Jonás, since it's through him I've discovered what separates me from my friends. And what makes me closer to him than to anyone else.

It's not that things didn't work with Ernesto. They were good years for both of us. Living with him was one of the best things I've ever done. I'll always love him. The loss of his father was a loss for me, too. But I think we always tend to look on the bright side of misfortune. The accident happened not long after we broke up, and not long after that I met Jonás. By then, there was a before and an after. An equator, a kind of phantom line. Maybe afterwards, at my lowest, I found a power, a strength. And the way we relate to everything, especially when it comes to love, changes after we hit rock bottom.

If this notebook had an ideal ending it would be a trip to the beach with Jonás. In the final lines I'd turn into a swallow, everything I've written would turn into a song and the notebook itself would take flight. Feathers would begin to sprout from Jonás' arms, his feet would gradually leave the sand and he'd start to fly. We'd be able to see our shadows on the water and together we'd hold a ribbon in the air that proclaimed *THE END*.

But no, it's not the end yet. And all this is too long to turn into a song. Jonás hasn't come back, this is a time of waiting and I'm Penelope. I weave, unravel, weave and unravel again. Will the day ever come when the waiting stops? Is there anyone who isn't waiting for something?

We're all waiting for something.

There's nothing like writing at midday on a Saturday while wearing slippers. It's a state very close to happiness. I'd be completely happy if I were also drinking a coffee and smoking a cigarette. We always need to be a few steps away from happiness. The transience of the state, the euphoria that can't last. Happiness is high-pitched. Like a woman talking in a high-pitched voice and everyone turning to look. It's such a good thing I stopped smoking, my slippers reassure me. My slippers are my state of mind, the embodiment of my soul.

I dreamed about sleeping with a stranger. When I woke up I didn't understand why the hell I'd gone off with him. As if my dream-life were a teenager running away from home. Who is that person I slept with?

I ask some questions about the future. Tepepunk answers me from Tokyo: 'In the future there's a pitch-black crow who makes a racket just before dawn each morning from his perch on a lamppost. His lamppost. Autumn's here at last, with its ochre-coloured winds. It really is pretty to see how the leaves crisp as the temperature drops, and how little by little a crunchy carpet covers the wide avenues. I don't want to sound cheesy, but I've been pondering the meaning of the seasons, the significance of the weather. Change, phases and movements. It makes me think about repetition and cycles, too. Things can never be the same, and yet that eternal return, clichéd as it is, marks out a rhythm in the series of variations that structures our experience of life. Here the seasons are clearly defined, signs of what's been and gone and what's yet to come. But they're not just beautiful landscapes; the present is also, as its name suggests, a gift. It doesn't suggest longing or loss. It's just a present, a gift, a time with no strings attached which is totally ours, to use however we want, however we please. There are days when I find the future overwhelming, with all the bright lights and commotion. The shops are the best museums, the best galleries and the Miyake or Yamamoto dresses are real works of art. As if that weren't enough, all the shops I go to are playing the music we listen to at home. Are we getting old? Becoming contemporary adults? Or does it just mean we have commercial tastes? Maybe when we're old we'll listen to the music they play in waiting rooms all over the world.'

My notebook is my waiting room. I write with background music. Maybe I should make an imperceptible playlist, like wallpaper, and turn all this into a proper waiting room. Perhaps lay out a few society magazines in this paragraph, with their stiff, wavy pages. A business weekly missing a cover, a gossip rag from a few years ago. So many people have flicked through these magazines. Maybe life is more like the waiting room than the doctor's surgery.

We talked about it last time, Jonás. If words behave like animals, stories can be divided into different kingdoms. Perhaps notebooks are a bit like dried butterflies on pins. I remember how in the waiting room at the dentist's I went to as a girl, there were some butterflies in a frame. A frame, some glass, protecting butterflies of different

89

sizes and colours. The waiting room is a concentration
of useless things. All the things we do to waste time. The
paraphernalia of uselessness, of lost time.

Is it possible to lose time?

An average of forty-one violent deaths a day in Mexico.
On the bloodiest days, sixty-nine. Sixty-nine names.
Sixty-nine stories. How many orphans, how many
partners, how many relatives? Each person's friends. Each
person's grief. The repercussions of the loss in their daily
life. The effects, the fears it unleashes. Sixty-nine stories
a day that set off, stampeding, kicking up dust, for the
red kingdom. Meanwhile, a politician tells his children –
while they're eating their bedtime cereal in the kitchen
– that he's had a tough day at work. The story of that
politician, one of the stories that belongs to the insect
kingdom.

This is a country that's waiting. Waiting for peace on the
streets, peace at bedtime. Here people are waiting for
safety – is that too much to ask?

Waiting, you say? Waiting for what, man?
Yeah, what are we waiting for, man?
What was that, man?
I was asking you, man – what are we waiting for?
But that's what I asked you.
Don't mess with me, man, I asked you.

I was hoping to be out of there as quickly as possible.
In the first stage of the recovery process, I had a tube
in my mouth that stopped me from speaking. I wrote
on a little pad of paper to communicate simple things
like 'Tell me about your day, go on'. For a couple of

weeks I couldn't say anything. One of the few decisions I made was not to let people turn the TV on. I didn't want to watch the news, or series, or anything like that. I wanted to know about the people who came to visit me, how they were, what they'd been up to. So all I could do was listen, think and write brief notes as a way of interacting. I couldn't physically read, and I didn't want to either, I wasn't even interested in reading. To hell with all that. During those days it was as if, despite all the reading and writing I'd done before, I was having the most beautiful linguistic experience of my life. A relationship beginning anew. Turning thirty, never questioning it, and then all of a sudden, right there in front of me: words in the full splendour of their everydayness, which can be used to sing a Shakira song, or so someone can tell you about their day. Words there, for listening to, for singing and telling. Listening; what bound me to those people and to everything else. Telling; what binds us together.

I'll tell you something, Jonás: today I went to the supermarket. They don't stock your favourite granola any more. It's true – I checked with the manager. I thought I'd take the opportunity to try something new. I bought a local brand of granola, in an eye-catching packet. It looks really delicious.

Tonight Guillermo came round with a shoebox to read me part of a novel he's writing on index cards. We drank beer and talked about a writer who promotes himself at every available opportunity. To a hilarious extent. We had fun going over some of his latest exploits. We agreed that the only thing left is for him to interview himself and then give himself a hug at the end.

It's eight-thirty a.m. I read the new granola packet. It's horrible, Jonás, a woman telling her story, in the first person, all about why she started making granola at home. The brand is named after her son, who disappeared in this pointless so-called War. A mother trying to raise money, through homemade granola, to fund a private investigation. I felt powerless, I lost my appetite. What the fuck is happening here?

It's eleven a.m. and Guillermo sends me an email with the subject 'Let's name the dwarf hippopotamus', and a link to an article: 'Lowry Park Zoo has organised a competition to name a pygmy hippo, which as the name suggests is much smaller than a normal hippo. It weighs 4.5 kilos and is 50 centimetres tall. It's estimated that globally, there are only around three hundred left in the wild. At present, the zoo is considering various names for this pygmy hippo, although the current front-runner is Greaseball.'

Juan José Arreola says hippos are like pensioners. Lounging placidly in their swamps, chewing slowly, wearing Hawaiian shorts and with cameras dangling around their necks. Guillermo suggests calling the pygmy pensioner Roberto.

Why this tendency of nature to make the same thing on different scales? If there's an average, then the variations, the bigger and smaller scales, are all different from one another. The further from the norm they are, the more misshapen.

Dwarf things. Small things. Little things in relation to the norm. Insignificant things. Things with different dimensions. Curiously, the stories I like the most are made up of trivialities. Details. Trifles. These days, people look to what's big. The big picture, big sales figures, success. Bright lights, interviews, breaking news. Whatever's famous. Importance judged by fame. Maybe small things are subversive. Living on a modest scale compared to the norm. Maybe the dwarf is the hero of our time.

On that short trip north, I talked to the girl who was writing a chapter of her thesis about Alberich. In Nordic mythology, dwarves were the creators of artifice. 'The origin of art, no more, no less,' she said with a smile.

The small as a bastion of the big. Perhaps that's how something might change. Especially in this country.

I'd like to go to the sea. I'd like the blue lines of this notebook to break, suddenly, like waves. To hear waves when I open this notebook, as if it were a music box.

13

This morning I walked past a café. I imagined Pessoa ordering five different drinks, one for each of his heteronyms. The girl would write the different names and specifications on each cup with a marker pen. I thought about that today. I suppose there are people who made better use of their time in that café. People with their computers, people chatting. Finalising editorial copy, studying, talking about work. A woman with wet hair sending messages from her phone, no doubt pulling the strings of an office.

Useful things. Useful work, useful thoughts, useful phrases. Stories in which everything happens. A society that worships the verb. The famous concept of utility, the pursuit of usefulness. The old story of separating the wheat from the chaff. If everything is divided into two, I'm on the side of the chaff. And oh, it smells so good.

I'm writing this by hand, but I wonder if fonts are facets of character. If Times New Roman says something about the people who use it, if Comic Sans would reveal something else. It suddenly seems like a lot of things fall within the semantic fields of fonts, and that we choose them because they resemble us in some way.

Jonás writes in Georgia, and I prefer Garamond. I have no reason for thinking this, but these fonts seem compatible, like the music we listen to. That's one good thing about living together – we're into more or less the same things. As I make myself something to eat, I'm going to listen to some Georgia-style music.

Listening to music has the power to dissolve tension. I wonder if this also applies in politics, if music can dissolve any kind of tension.

Misfortune, difficulties and obstacles have value. Difficult times make you look inside yourself. Make you listen and observe. Hardship can be transformed into strength. I wonder if this applies to politics too, if disaster can become social strength.

I ate in the Japanese restaurant with Carolina. I saw another dwarf; she was having dinner with a man. I smiled at her.

This evening I went for a walk in the park with Luis Felipe. He's so good to talk to. In his opinion, Jonás is trying hard to be 'the good son' in the wake of his mother's death.

I wish I'd met Jonás at a different time. Grief has a protagonist and a host of minor characters. The protagonist is the one who suffers, like Jonás. Deep down, he thinks he's misunderstood. He shares part of it with his sister, and part of it with his father, but there's something he doesn't know how to express, and he keeps that from everyone. He's the protagonist, and I'm secondary. That's why his return is being postponed.

Sometimes I wonder if being with me is, for Jonás, a kind of betrayal of his mother. On a basic level, perhaps it's not such a crazy idea. If he does feel that way, it explains why he's putting off coming back. I don't know. Still, here I am, Jonás, and maybe I'm thinking all this like a cat getting tangled in a ball of wool.

Instead of the ball of wool, I should pick up an actual ball. The texture of objects that bounce: one of my favourite stories is about the first ever writing. Ovid's *Metamorphoses* contains the first writer and the first writing. Io is the daughter of the Inachus river. Juno turns Io into a beautiful white cow. When she wants to complain to Argus – who watches her with his hundred eyes – all she does is moo. She's terrified by her own voice, by that moo. She realises she can't speak. She can't communicate with her father, the Inachus river. Instead of words she uses letters, tracing them with her hoof in the sand to explain how her body was transformed. The father realises it's his daughter and laments.

The first thing ever written down is a lament. The first writer writes the lament of her transformation. The first writing is on sand, on the banks of a river; words that soon become indistinct, that don't last. Io, a woman transformed into a cow, writes her misfortune. *Io* is also, in Italian, 'I'. The first person. The first person wrote her misfortune. With a woman's cry of distress, that's how writing began.

Before Cervantes, the first novel was written by a woman in Japan in the tenth century. A cry of distress in Japanese in an age when Chinese was the high language, that's what Murasaki created. *The Tale of Genji* is the first novel. Love in the time of Genji could transform love today.

Sor Juana also wrote in that strange and newly-minted language of New Spain. Io wrote for the first time in sand. Three women transformed the word.

If I had an AM radio show, I'd talk about them more. If I had a show in the early hours, I'd read something by them. It was Tania who said we should have a radio show, the AM kind where the words sound fuzzy. We'd introduce a few songs, make long phonecalls live on air. Not much music, but all love songs. Like the one I'm humming now, my friends.

I'm so comfortable that I'm going to get a book. Now I'm back, with who else but Little Flower, the smallest woman in the world, from Clarice Lispector's story: 'In the Central Congo he indeed discovered the smallest pygmies in the world. And – like a box within a box, within a box – among the smallest pygmies in the world was the smallest of the smallest pygmies in the world, obeying perhaps the need Nature sometimes has to outdo herself.'

Today I saw the other dwarf again, walking down the street. I saw her go into a pharmacy. The one who was in the Japanese restaurant the other day. I noticed her flowery dress. A very feminine look. A modest neckline, but it left her collarbones visible, and the beginnings of her breasts. The cut showed off her figure, she looked very beautiful. A woman's dress but in a small size, a child's size?

As a girl I never wanted a dog; I was more into cats. I remember waiting ages until I was allowed to have a cat at home. I had to wait until everyone agreed, until my brother was on board, until the vet would let us adopt one. The whole thing took so long that, by the time the cat arrived, I had a list of names ready. My first cat had three names.

It feels like we're always waiting for something. However small, however trivial it might seem. An endless wait, the carrot always ahead of us. And the names ready for when it comes. If it comes.

While I've been waiting, perhaps Jonás, like the dwarf, has stopped looking like Jonás. Perhaps now he's an idea. An ideal. Which is what they both are for me, what everything is for me.

Waiting. It never starts, never ends. We never arrive. We arrive somewhere, somewhere like Lisbon, but never at a conclusion. Or we arrive, no matter what, at these words: 'All is truth and way.'

Everything begins once something else has already begun. My name and my story don't begin with my birth. A story doesn't end with death or a farewell. The other people are still there, the ones from before, the ones who carry on, the ones who are here now. Like Jonás, like me, the two of us on the way, at the end of something and the beginning of something else.

Like me, now, waiting for Jonás to come back from his trip. But even if he does come back, it's possible his journey will continue. Charon clearly doesn't just take the chosen one; for every trip to Hades, several planes take off from the airport. That journey in search of someone, of something that's not there. Or that journey without flying. Like this one here, in the chair.

I wonder what the planets are like that the cat visits in his sleep. Like a box within a box, within a box, where does the cat travel to?

I'd live with you on any of those nine little planets, Jonás. The black cat could be the emperor of one of them. On that planet, there'd be a garden decorated with different-size pieces of quartz, in different shades of green, with a small pale-blue frozen lake we'd like to visit. The emperor Cat would learn that we enjoy strolling among the huge rocks of quartz, that black cat who watches us from his throne; he'd lick his paw and flex it to order the garden's closure. 'It's mine,' he'd say to his subjects. 'No one else may walk between my rocks of quartz,' he'd decree. We'd obey the orders in his kingdom, just as we obey them at home. We'd look for another place. It wouldn't have different-size pieces of quartz in different shades of green, or a pale-blue frozen lake, but it would be a place we'd like to go to on the little planet the cat might visit in his sleep.

Maybe all this could be put another way, but if there's no ideal person there are no ideal words. So there can be no ideal story.

14

A message from Ernesto, inviting me for lunch. Nothing out of the ordinary, though we don't see each other very much. The only thing that really was out of the ordinary today was my doughnut sliding across my plate. I don't know what effect, what optical illusion or law of physics allowed it, but it happened: the doughnut slid across the plate. I wonder if things like that happen on one of the planets the cat visits in his sleep, something like a planet where things move of their own accord. In keeping with the laws of that planet, the notebook would levitate now. On one of those planets, objects would have a mind of their own. Objects would have a voice.

A long phone conversation with my brother. He said he'd like to have a cat but he can't because his girlfriend is allergic, and then he took a different tack: 'And if you had seven lives like a cat, what would you want to be? If I had seven lives I'd divide them into seven months, one month for each person. First I'd be a shaman from Chiapas, can you imagine? Then I'd be a country singer from Kansas, and sell cowboy hats − I have a flannel shirt that would be just perfect. And a teenager in Tokyo. I'd have so many friends, you wouldn't believe, and I'd be shit-hot on a skateboard. And a kid on a beach in Michoacán, preferably drinking from a coconut through a straw while sitting at a plastic table; and a children's party magician in Buenos Aires; and an old Scottish man no one would understand a word of when he spoke; and someone selling coffee in the market in Oaxaca. Have you smelt the freshly ground coffee in that market? Wouldn't it be amazing? Seriously, sis, I want to come back to Mexico soon. Did you notice I chose various people in Mexico?'

At this moment, the cat's engaged in an epic battle with the label from the bread. Adapting Kafka for cats, it seems that in the struggle between the cat and the label, we have to take the side of the label.

I wrote the last few entries lying in bed. I wonder if this position leads to different sentences than those written in a chair or standing up or in a taxi or on a bus or walking along. Either way, I still need to try writing in my sleep.

Proust used to write lying down. The black cat is rarely in any other position. Maybe the little planets he travels to in his sleep are in the Proust Galaxy.

Something happened in the street today. It was around noon and I was walking along the pavement. At the traffic lights, a taxi driver was shouting abuse at a woman who'd stopped him turning where it wasn't allowed. 'Motherfucking bitch,' the taxi driver yelled. The woman turned off the engine of her SUV, looked at the taxi driver and got out in a rage. 'For your information,' she said, 'my mother died recently, and it was very sad for my siblings and me, so show some respect. Besides, that's no way to talk to a woman. Maybe you never had a mother to teach you manners at home. And why did you swear at me? Just because you wanted to turn where it's not allowed? Don't you have a wife? Or daughters? You obviously never talk to women, if that's how you treat them.' When she'd finished, two or three people gave her a smattering of applause. By then, several curious bystanders had gathered, among them a plump policeman from a pharmacy, who was the first person to clap. The woman went back to her car. A man asked if she'd like him to punch the taxi driver who'd offended her. She closed the door, as if bidding farewell to the crowd. A driver honked his horn, as if giving the woman an ovation.

We may not all be parents, but we are all children. Perhaps this obvious fact was what prompted the general empathy with the woman. Perhaps it was also her courage and eloquence. And what would happen if every time someone offended a woman, she responded along those lines?

I wonder if our position in relation to our parents marks our character. If that woman, if that taxi driver, if Jonás or I are what we are because of where we are in relation to our parents. As if the members of a family formed a figure, a simple shape, like a rectangle, a cross or a circle. And we form that shape simply because we exist in relation to other people. I also wonder if the taxi driver's insults, and his attempt to turn in the wrong place, are a sign of something bigger in this country. As if there's an enormous whale swimming in the depths of the ocean and all we see is the odd bubble bursting on the surface, like that scene in the street.

The problem with this place. What is the problem with this place? There's no one verb that can sum it up. There are so many. Several of those verbs are all over the press every day. Even though Spanish syntax shouldn't let them, they insist, the verbs, in jostling to the front of the headlines. They even contort, the verbs, as if in a circus, on a tightrope, to be the most important words in the newspaper headlines.

Isn't the role of verbs interesting? The verbs that denote action, what's happening here and now. They're like the little hands on a clock, they tell you the exact time in sentences. Whereas waiting, like the clock in the dentist's surgery, could have the minute hand stopped or the second hand skipping. Waiting renders verbs useless. Sentences without verbs, like cutting a puppet's strings. Nothing moves. On the contrary. In the waiting something is paused: the verbs are like ornaments. And the verb 'wait' looks very similar to a sofa. Oh, those big fluffy cushions.

I bought a floor cleaner called Poet. Today I cleaned the kitchen with Poet. The apartment smells nice, if a bit sweet. Which is what you'd expect if you use poetry to do your housework, though the moment poets have the same task as disinfectant, something's gone wrong. My mother, for example, would never buy a cleaning fluid called Poet; a product called Action would be more up her street. She'd see the word Poet as a nuisance, like some inherited furniture she'd have declared useless and thrown out long ago given half a chance. My mother would have got rid of poetry just like every summer she got rid of things she considered unusable from the cupboard my brother and I shared. Our choice of cleaning products shows how we're different. I bought Poet, with the scent of wild flowers, because it seemed like the epitome of everything I hate most about poetry.

A long conversation about Poet floor cleaner with Luis Felipe. He read me some verses that, in his opinion, are classics of the floor-cleaner genre. 'This guy is like a Jehovah's Witness of rhyme,' he said. We reached the point where his laughter was making me laugh. Before hanging up, I told him how much I loved him.

I think I end phone calls to my friends with a whiff of Poet.

Insomnia. To slow my brain down I went to get the notebook. It wasn't easy to find. I don't know how it moved from the table where I thought I left it. Could the cat have done it from one of the little planets he visits in his sleep? Or has it acquired the same powers as the doughnut that slid across the plate? It was down the side of the armchair, under the cushion, where I also found one of Jonás' socks. And maybe it had the effect of the skull on Hamlet: with the sock on my hand I thought that Jonás, even if he comes back from his trip, will never really come back. Sometimes I get tired of waiting. What am I waiting for? Am I waiting for Jonás to come home or am I waiting for him to share what's going on? His journey to Spain has taken me on another journey. Twenty thousand leagues under the notebook, this journey I'm making from my chair while Jonás is away.

I'm not sure I like you tonight, Jonás. It's a good thing you're not here. If you were here, I'd sleep on the sofa. I'm arguing with you even though you're not here. What's more, I'm still on the sofa.

Have I said that my notebook is ideal, among other things, because I can use it as a coaster? To write this, I've had to put my morning coffee mug on the table. Since the table's made of wood, the mug leaves white rings on it. There are various rings, like the ghosts of other times, other mugs.

If I close the notebook and rest my mug of hot coffee on it, it will be doing one of its many jobs. The notebook is a bit like a freelancer. So I'll stop writing. Ideally the notebook could show off all its functions at once.

This afternoon, after a family lunch, I went for a walk. Between Calle Londres and Calle Lisboa – that mysterious intersection where I felt like I'd encountered my granddad and my brother – is the Wax Museum. A disconcerting place, a museum with nothing museum-like about it; it's more like a cult of celebrity. Among the famous wax figures, I found Snow White and the seven dwarves. The dwarves came up to my knee. I was disappointed, they seemed too dwarf-like. In the art section I took a photo with Lautrec. The same height as the dwarf on the block, but less elegant.

Tania told me about Catalina, an Italian art collector who lives in the Condesa neighbourhood. She came to Mexico City in the seventies. Apparently she has a castle in Italy, an apartment in New York and various other properties elsewhere, but the big house in Condesa is her base. She married a Mexican artist who died in the eighties, and after that she decided to stay in Mexico. 'Most of all,' said Tania, 'she has pots of money and an eclectic collection, with a line that supports young artists. Rumour has it she's short, partly because she's shrunk with age and partly because she's the product of an incestuous relationship between two Italian aristocrats. But I think it gives her character. Plus she's a force of nature, she'll be sitting in her Louis XV armchair – her feet don't even touch the floor – and then all of a sudden she'll hop down mid-sentence, ring a little bell and a maid will come along to show you out. "I'm fed up with you," she'll say to your face, and the maid will escort you to the door. She has the spirit of Alexander the Great, you know what I mean?' I'd like to meet Catalina.

I've been left with a psychological tic. Suddenly I'm scared of death. Suddenly I'm scared that I'll lie down, go to sleep and everything will be over. I'm scared of the end. Suddenly I'm scared of the dark. Of that being it, with no Shakira songs to wake me. I like being here so much that I don't want it to end. The time will come, but I like being here. I want to be here. More than that, I love it. I don't want to know when the end will come and I don't want to know what tomorrow will bring because I love being here now. It's strange: when I see things this clearly I stop being scared, because it's this, this being here, this moment which is happening now, and which begins to fade as soon as I write anything, and which is luckily followed by this one, and this one, and then this other moment that's as full of life as the next.

Sometimes I sing while I'm doing the washing up. Sometimes I dance while I'm cooking, or in the living room while I'm sweeping the floor. If I put music on, I normally end up singing in the living room. Time to turn this song up, it's so good.

I saw a boy in the street wearing a Pinocchio T-shirt. I remembered the time in the Japanese restaurant when we talked about the origins of our names. You told me you saw *Pinocchio* with Marina and your mother in a cinema that doesn't exist any more – the one with the façade like a castle, where my brother and I used to be taken as well, and which was knocked down to make way for a shopping mall. And I remember you saying your mother liked the name's biblical history. 'But how awful,' you said, 'to be trapped inside a big fish.'

Is mourning like being trapped inside a big fish?

Let's read the Bible like it's a horoscope for names. Let's see, let's see. Yahweh speaks to Jonah, tells him to go to Nineveh, a big city, to announce its impending destruction. Jonah doesn't want to go. He runs away. He wants to go to Tarshish instead, to escape Yahweh. He gets onto a boat to travel far away. Tarshish is far away, it's at the end of the world. Jonah, in the boat, wants to escape as far away as he can, and Tarshish seems like a good place to escape to. But Yahweh unleashes a storm at sea, so violent it looks like the ship might sink. Jonah is sound asleep, the sailors are afraid. From the storm and the rocking of the ship, they deduce that Jonah is running away from Yahweh and they blame him for the storm. They wake him up. How can they calm the sea's rage? Jonah tells the sailors to throw him overboard: they do it and the waters settle. Yahweh makes a big fish swallow Jonah up. Inside the belly of the fish, Jonah realises he can't escape. Jonah spends three days and three nights in the fish's stomach. From the heart of the sea, he speaks to Yahweh. The deep closed around me, weeds were wrapped around my head, the earth closed behind me forever, says Jonah from the stomach of the big fish. Jonah repents and Yahweh orders the fish to vomit Jonah out.

Can you swim?

15

Last night I went to a party in a big house. The Most Important Artist in Mexico showed up in a tiny Coca-Cola-coloured car. Every so often, his driver came in with bottles, food and other bits and pieces, which he placed decorously on the table. While the artist was talking to a woman in a sequinned dress, the driver passed him a little packet of cigarettes and something that, from where we were, looked like a yellow bath sponge. Guillermo, mezcal in hand, made up a conversation in which the artist convinced the woman how useful and how thoroughly appropriate it was to have a sponge at a party.

And what if the three nights Jonah spends inside the big fish are the equivalent of three years? I hope not. The apartment feels too big for me when you're not here, just like the days do.

After our phone call, I think you might be having a better time. Less guilty, less anxious, less afraid. I hope you've calmed down a bit, I want to listen to you better. Before I go and have a shower, I can tell you that I wish you'd been at that party with Guillermo and me last night, but I don't know what else I can tell you. Sometimes you trap me in these alleyways, and I don't know how to get out.

This afternoon I bought some earrings. Two swallows. I'm wearing them now, one swallow on each side.

I'm listening to the end of the national anthem, during the National Hour, which is my favourite time on a Sunday. Although I don't normally listen to this programme and I don't know these verses, I'm not going to change it. Like when people used to think the world was flat and boats would fall off the edge into the abyss, it's as if nothing comes after the final verses of the national anthem on a Sunday evening. My brother has a catchphrase for when he forgets something: 'The maps!' It comes from a moment one Sunday evening when he remembered he had to buy maps, or cardboard, or something like that from the stationer's.

There's a strange verb in the national anthem. Here, under the microscope: *osare*. To dare in the future subjunctive, a verbal tense that's now extinct, like the dodo. Those verbal contortions that used to exist and can now only be found in glass cabinets, displayed in songs from other eras like museum exhibits. At the same time, there are so many kinds of music, and so many new songs born every hour, that perhaps nine words are born into the world every day.

Don't ask how I got here, I don't know how I got here, but when the film *Snow White* won an award, it wasn't given one statue but seven miniature versions: one for each dwarf. Oh, I just love this limbo time on a Sunday evening. The seven days setting off into the distance in single file, whistling the same tune.

I love listening to the radio, especially on Sundays. Just like in the street, there's less traffic, less noise. Today they played a Beatles song I didn't know, and I listened to it with my mother in the living room at home. Now I remember that Ana also liked The Beatles. I wonder if my mother and Ana stood in the same queue at the university library, if their paths crossed, if they exchanged the odd phrase, greeting or glance in their student days.

While I was recovering, one night we talked about the music she listened to when she was younger. With some four or five groups, and perhaps a few other hits, my mother would have everything she needs to describe her youth. I remember her singing in the kitchen, making coffee, smoking a menthol cigarette. I remember her slipping out of tune now and then, happily singing away.

I asked if she liked the song they played on the radio. Pushing her a little more, even though The Beatles are one of the buttons that switch her past on right away: 'Oh, but that's one of the most mediocre Beatles songs, sweetheart. No, I don't like it at all. As I've said before, we had a portable record player because my dad didn't let us use his, the one in the living room. I was five or six and I remember that whenever my brothers and sisters put a Beatles record on I'd bounce up and down on the armchairs – I'm talking about 1964, sweetheart – and when my brother turned up the volume I'd take my shoes off, throw the cushions in the air and dance until my mum came in and told us to calm down. I remember my parents talking at the dinner table about those "shaggy-haired" guys who came along to wreak havoc with their "noise". My father called them Las Beatles instead of Los Beatles, that's right, with the feminine article, because they had long hair and back then it was very eccentric to have long hair. You can imagine. Anyway, while my dad went on criticising them in the kitchen at home,

The Beatles were really taking off. They were played on the radio more and more. I grew up listening to that music. When I was at secondary school, they were in a real hippy phase – this is the start of the seventies I'm talking about, when they recorded that famous album, *Bangladesh*. It was a really expensive record. Listen, I'll tell you all about it. One time when I was bunking off school with my friends, we went to a shop called Hip 70 where they sold imported records – oh, Mexico City was completely different in those days, you'd be amazed if you could see La Telaraña, the clothes shop, or boutique, as they were called then, or our official menu of *molletes* and coffee in the VIPS in Altavista, or the bowling alley we went to, which is a supermarket now, but anyway, that shop stocked the precious record and we hid it in the hippie satchel my friend Hugo brought me back from Oaxaca, the one my mother found so embarrassing. We strolled nonchalantly out of the shop with the record in the satchel. There were six of us, we were in hysterics about having left with the record without anyone realising and we carried on to Hugo's house to listen to our new acquisition. Yes, sweetheart, we stole it. But "Michelle" and "With a Little Help from My Friends" are my favourite songs because when I started going to parties with my sisters when I was fourteen, fifteen, your only chance of getting anywhere near the boy you liked was if he asked you to dance one of those slow songs "cheek to cheek". And I thought "Michelle" was such a lovely song at that age. But my teenage years, as you know, were coloured by a lot of fraught moments and confrontations with my parents. We were always at odds; they couldn't stand so many of the things I liked, you see. It was a different time, sweetheart, all those Catholic exiles struggling to uphold the morals of their large families. They hit me a fair bit and we had plenty of arguments, my mother and I most of all, and on top of that their generation just didn't understand anything. I remember one afternoon perfectly, how I felt so understood and so loved, singing "With a Little Help from My Friends" with those six friends of mine at the age of sixteen, in my friend Hugo's living room. So, you see, they pulled that song out of the hat to make money with the name of the group that meant everything to my generation. But it's nothing like the classics we sang when we were sixteen.'

I remember Jonás describing one of his last afternoons with his mother. She asked him to work out a Beatles song on the piano. Jonás isn't good at working out music by ear. He told me they were listening to the same song over and over again until he could figure out the beginning. 'Night fell. There was a power cut, it was a really weird moment. As if the electricity going was a sign that she'd be gone soon too. Yeah. I couldn't see her, but I could hear her. She was lighting candles in the kitchen, humming the part that came next, the part I couldn't work out on the piano, kind of helping me.'

One Saturday, not long after we moved in together, Jonás went for a run in the park. Completely unexpectedly, he heard the song he'd been trying to work out on the piano that afternoon. He took his headphones out and started crying right there in the park. The first time he'd cried since Ana's death. He came home. After a while, leaning against the fridge, he told me what had happened: 'Crazy, right? It's only hit me now that my mum's not here any more. Don't you realise, darling? She's not here. My mum's gone.' He described that afternoon to me in detail, one of his last afternoons with his mother. By the end we were both in tears.

My mum, so as not to cry, so as to dispel that memory, to shake off that moment at which she'd felt so loved at the age of sixteen, described her shock when, not long after getting married, while listening to the radio in that little cream-coloured car they used to have, she heard the news that John Lennon had been killed.

16

I was left with a scar. I think telling stories is a way of putting a scar into words. Since not all blows or falls leave marks, the words are there, ready to be put together in different ways, anywhere, anytime, in response to any fall, however serious or slight.

17

We don't have a TV, but we do have a neighbour who takes it upon herself to share the evening news with us all at full blast. Through the wall, I learn that ninety-five per cent of cases involving murdered journalists are unresolved.

Are we getting closer or are we getting further away?

I had dinner with Julia. Calmly, while eating a salad, she said that we usually want something and think we're heading towards it, when really we're walking in the opposite direction. I think it's a powerful claim. Could it be what's happening to this country? Could it be what's happening to me?

Am I getting closer or am I getting further away?

I forgot to say that yesterday this notebook came in useful for turning off the light. I stretched out my arm but couldn't reach the switch, and yet thanks to the notebook's solidarity we managed it together, in a true bilateral partnership. As you can see, the notebook, reproduced and widely distributed, could serve as political discourse. And thrown at the right moment it could be an anarchist gesture.

My father is a private person. I find talking to him quite tough. He can be difficult to approach, and he doesn't like to open up. His younger brother is seriously ill, and it looks like he won't live much longer. A horrible shock. My brother phoned; he said our cousin had called him to pass on the news. He sent me on ahead, like when we were children, to test the waters. I called just now. 'How are you?' I asked. After I'd put the same question to him several times, he answered: 'Oh, fine, love, just working as usual. Nothing to report, except my brother Ricardo's not doing so well, so why don't you tell me about your day?' Talking to him reminded me of his illegible handwriting.

Tania is having relationship problems: 'It's a mess. And you know what? The cold doesn't help. I don't think we'll last much longer. Plus, I'm sure the weather has a lot to do with it. Always, with everything. I bet if we were at the beach we wouldn't be arguing so much. Plus, if we were at the beach, instead of fighting we'd have made a ceviche or maybe sat on the porch and played cards. Have you seen that? Doesn't it look tempting? A couple in flip-flops, chatting away on plastic chairs outside their house, the hundred-watt bulb, the bag of water hung up to scare off the flies. That's how my life would be if I lived by the beach. Today I'd have said to him, "Give me a hand moving the hammock," instead of hanging up on him. I don't remember where I heard that things have a tendency to end in winter. Statistics, percentages that prove things end more often in winter than in summer. And we all think we're different, but we're part of the statistics. Even though no one wants to be part of the statistics.'

Maybe the winter, the cold, the leaves on the ground, are related to the end. *Like a leaf clings to the tree.* But please don't let it end, Jonás. *With your kiss my life begins.*

The doctor said I had to go for walks and get some sun. 'Like an old person, walking round the block?' I asked. The doctor, who's in his seventies, smiled: 'Plants, and you, and everyone else, get strength from sunlight. You're just nicer-looking than a plant, so you might as well go outside. If you were ugly I'd suggest only going out at night so you don't scare people, but I think it's ok, you can go out during the day. You'll recover in no time, just you wait. The day you stop to buy some sorbet, that'll be it, the next day you'll be going for a run.'

I'd just moved in with Jonás. We went to a party with his friends. We were kissing. The music was terrible, like at the end of a wedding. When I say we were kissing I mean that from there we went home, that we weren't embarrassed and that if any of his friends had seen us at home they would have seen the same thing as at the party. It never used to be like that. Before, being around friends, around other people, seemed to alter the situation. But with Jonás it was different. Something changed. Living together made us feel more comfortable. The setting doesn't matter. The trip, the distance, doesn't affect that. I don't think there's any embarrassment or shyness between us, although, now I think about it, perhaps silence is a kind of shyness. It's strange, at home I never thought there was any embarrassment or shyness between us.

The first time I cooked for Jonás in the apartment we'd soon be sharing, he was anxious, wanting to help. I asked him not to, to let me cook for him, to talk to me about something while I cooked. In the end he started chopping next to me. It's rare for Jonás not to help me in the kitchen. It sounds silly, but that minor gesture encapsulates a lot of things about him, on a larger scale, and it's part of what made me fall in love with him. Jonás can't be in the same place as someone without helping, without offering some kind of support. He enjoys working as a team, like when he brings crosswords home for us to solve together. The very thing that made me fall in love with him is also what's keeping us apart. Now he's by his mother's side. How can I bring him back?

Sometimes we do crosswords. He introduced them, I've never bought any of those publications. One Sunday, visiting his father and sister, I learnt something. 'I don't like them,' Marina said in their living room while Jonás and his father were taking things out of the car boot. Ana liked doing crosswords, and Jonás used to help her ever since he was a boy. 'I was never part of that, crosswords bore me to death,' Marina said.

It feels like the sun is making things better, like the warm weather is helping. Summer in Mexico City doesn't go in a straight line. The same day can switch between baking heat and a storm. The next morning can be the other way around, or take a different course altogether. The same day can tie the two ends of the rope together. I was born in summer, and if I had to choose a static horoscope, a single defining statement, I'd choose this description from Shakespeare of the summer in Mexico City: 'Welcome. A hundred thousand welcomes! I could weep, and I could laugh; I am light, and heavy. Welcome!' From one extreme to the other, everything can change in a flash. Just like after an accident, and just like when I met Jonás. One day you're here, and the next you're over there. Because, oh, Wild is the Wind.

Could night and day be a dwarf model of winter and summer? It seems more plausible for a relationship to end at night than at midday. I imagine it's easier to get into an argument in the middle of the night. For the leaf, hanging from the tree, to fall in the cold. Perhaps death also has something wintry about it. It looks like a family winter is on the way, but I have a feeling my father will stay standing. If he breaks like a branch I'd like him to lean on us, on my brother and me, but for that he'd have to be open with us, which I can't imagine. Sometimes I wonder if men's emotions are like a closed box somewhere in the distance, so far into the distance that the distance is where they are. I wonder if they're illegible. But if you can't stop the winter, can you delay the following summer? Oh, tell me, Jonás, when will the sun come out?

I went for lunch with Ernesto. It was nice to see him. At one point he said that the most violent men are often short: 'It makes sense, maybe in self-defence they turn into the bastards who push everyone else around. There's Napoleon, who was the size of this salt cellar. Remember my brother's boss? Another tyrant, he's been one since primary school. And what about the cartel boss they caught yesterday, did you see on the news? The man's a midget. Or our diminutive president, who always appears in cartoons in a suit three sizes too big. Being too tall has the opposite effect. That was one of my dad's theories, he said people who are too tall bumble around like big dogs.'

Yesterday I realised I'm coming to the end of this Ideal notebook and went out to look for some more. Needless to say, I didn't find any. In an old stationery shop in the Escandón I found a notebook from around the same time. The name of the brand is Atlántida. It has the figure of Atlas on it, along with the slogan 'Guarantee and quality'; those words, in rounded text, form a world that the person is carrying on his back. One good thing about Ideal notebooks is that they don't have slogans. Ideal things are ideal in the eye of the reader, like a mirror-word, a natural word that reflects us. In another, even older stationery shop, I found some notebooks that are similar to Ideal ones. I bought two. I wonder which one is the imitation of the other.

I had some mezcal with Philippe and Luis Felipe. Mario turned up; he was on his way to another table, but he sat with us for a while. According to him, the other, similar notebooks are older than the Ideals. 'How do you know?' 'Because a man in a stationery shop in Roma told me,' he answered. I described the conversation with the old lady in the stationer's in Oaxaca. We swapped stories about things we've been told by people in stationery shops. I gave him one of the notebooks I had in my rucksack.

I also bought an old-style pen with a fine tip. This pen feels more comfortable to write with than the last one. Like a pair of made-to-measure shoes. I can run – see? And I can write more quickly, look how well I'm doing at this speed. I'm running. Oh, look, I'm messing up my hair. And I can write whatever I want without stopping because this nib suits the size of my writing. Oh, it's amazing, I've found my ideal pen.

18

It's a Sunday evening, my very favourite time to listen to the radio, but I'm going to turn it off. The neighbour's listening to some pretty good music, turned up pretty loud, so I'll leave the playlist to him. I've just been to see Jonás' father and sister; they invited me over for dinner. In amongst all the joking around, they tried to justify his behaviour, like they were asking me to be patient. The truth is, it's stopped mattering how much time goes by. This armchair is getting more and more comfortable, and it's even better now the neighbour's playing such good music.

After all, we're both on a journey. But I prefer to travel by armchair. Although I could argue from here, I don't like arguing, I prefer the journeys I can make sitting down. Oh, those two big themes, the poems that produced us: the poem of war, and the poem of a journey. *The Iliad* and *The Odyssey*. Maybe everything can be divided like that, into the *Iliad* side and the *Odyssey* side. *The Iliad* was named after a city. *The Odyssey* was named after a character. The horizontal poem like a postcard, the vertical poem like a full-length portrait. I prefer *The Odyssey*. We both look more like our mother, *The Odyssey*. Me like Penelope, and you like Odysseus.

Odysseus, he of the many twists and turns. Penelope, she of the many twists and turns without moving from her armchair. Weaving the notebook by day and unravelling it at night. Our Telemachus is the black cat stretching on the floor. He doesn't seem about to go looking for Jonás. Our Telemachus yawns, licks one paw with his eyes closed and it's all the same to him whether Jonás comes back or I leave. If only someone, like he whose voice is borne afar, could tell the cat that he does matter to us, that we love him.

The neighbour has just played that song I love again. Because of his good taste and his tendency to repeat things, I offer him some questions as if they were biscuits: what would have happened if Odysseus had been a dwarf? Would it have changed *The Odyssey*, the course of the West?

Does our height determine our destiny? Do scales determine history?

If our scale determines the role we play in history, it must mean something that Jonás and I are the same height. Face to face, in similar circumstances, interaction is easier. At similar points, as if what we've been through matches up. After all, his travels in Spain and my travels in the armchair run parallel.

Sometimes I'd like to know this story from start to finish, but I don't know anything from start to finish. Even my handwriting, on the page in front of me, looks like a film I've walked into once the screening's already begun. It used to be big, and now it's smaller, but that's still not the beginning. Does it look like my father's handwriting, my mother's, my grandparents'? One good thing about narratives in the past tense is that you can synthesise and select, because you know the story from start to finish. If this were written in the past, if a divine narrator were talking, like he whose voice is borne afar, we could have epithets the way they do in *The Odyssey*. It would make things easier. The qualities, the defects, would be obvious, and there would be clues. Since I don't have any clues, since this is the present and it looks more like an annotated margin, I can offer some epithets that only depict an instant. I could be she of the small handwriting, and Julia could be she who shyly plays guitar. And then there's landline-calling Tania, golden-shoed Carolina. Or some obvious adjectives: Guillermo the intelligent, Tepepunk the tall, Antonio the sharp, Luis Felipe the divine.

They say we look like one or the other, that either the maternal or paternal features are dominant. I look more like my mother, and my brother looks more like my father. Jonás looks like his mother and Marina looks like their father. Ana was an attractive woman, with black hair, light-coloured eyes and dark, full eyebrows. Those dominant features in Jonás attracted me the day we met. I feel drawn to *The Odyssey*, and perhaps the literature I like the most shares its qualities.

They respond, they agree. Proust, Wilde, Pessoa, Borges and Lispector love *The Odyssey*. Juan Rulfo, Jorge Ibargüengoitia and Josefina Vicens say they do too, that they're big fans. Oh, the Ouija notebook.

I said just now that this is a margin. In fact, that's what I do and what I've been doing all this time: I make notes in the margins of books. It's hard to make notes when the margins are too narrow: that's why I buy notebooks. This notebook is also one long margin of everything I like to read.

And isn't sitting in an armchair a way of reading life?

As a teenager, I didn't put up posters in my bedroom. Something keeps me from that kind of celebrity worship. Besides, I worship the margins, the secondary, the useless. And in an age when a pet can become a celebrity, an age of epic stories, of tales that have to be grand and flashy to capture a child's attention, an age when preference is given to speed and usefulness, what's a good reason to fly that flag?

Kafka, come here: 'There is no need for you to leave the house. Stay at your table and listen. Don't even listen, just wait. Don't even wait, be completely quiet and alone. The world will offer itself to you to be unmasked; it can't do otherwise; in raptures it will writhe before you.'

I spoke to Antonio the other day. He has some new nicknames for a person we both think is awful. So funny. It put me in a good mood and I went out to buy something for dinner. On the way, I ran into Luis Felipe. We had tacos at a place by the park.

What would become of a person with no friends?

My neck hurts. If my notebook had a detachable page that I could use as a heat patch, it would be ideal.

Wait. I love this song. The neighbour has such good taste. It's true, writing is more like unravelling than weaving. Unravelling involves having woven something already and there's always so much to unravel. But I won't take out the part about the neighbour. What great choices. I'm singing along.

The Odyssey has a happy ending. But I wonder what's in store here, what's in store here for the two of us. Come back, so everything can carry on happily. We'll resume our domestic life. Since they stopped making the granola you used to like, we'll see which one we like now.

I read, in an essay, that one of Flann O'Brien's *Irish Times* columns described a strange service for the owners of unopened books: 'For a given sum the books would be handled; passages would be underlined, the spines would be damaged or words would be written in the margins such as "Rubbish" or "Yes, but cf Homer, Od., iii, 151" or "I remember poor Joyce saying the very same thing to me", or inscriptions would be added to the first page along the lines of "From your devoted friend and follower, K. Marx".'

Marginal, useless work. In fact, I'm drawn to the very idea of uselessness because there's something almost fictional about it. A piece of work, an object, the more ridiculously useless it seems, the more fascinating I find it. All those objects, all those services that serve no one seem to me like the triumph of fiction. How I'd like to offer the book-underlining service, write in the margins, add false dedications, drink coffee, and now and then leave marks on the covers with my mug.

The more useless something is, the more subversive.

Let me unravel that.

The more useless something is, the more independent it is from reality.

It's the music. It's the neighbour's music, the bus driving by, the aeroplane in the distance, a dog barking here, a car horn over there. I'd like to be a sound so I could contribute to the night. If I were a sound I could be independent from reality. If I were music I could travel further.

I didn't tell you something when we talked just now. The other day I had lunch with Carolina and some of her friends. One of them took a notebook out of her bag and put it on the table. An Ideal notebook. 'I call them Mexican Moleskines,' she said. I picked it up and had a look. It was a bit smaller than the ones I found in Oaxaca. I asked her where she'd bought it. She gave me the address of a stationer's in the centre which had – she said – a green Ideal notebook in the window: 'But don't get too excited, I thought they had them in green, which is my favourite colour, but no, it's just faded in the sun. Really they only sell navy-blue Ideal notebooks, but since the man in the shop's always in a bad mood he won't show you any. If you look at the spine you can tell it was blue once upon a time.' I thought about that Ideal notebook as a kind of mummified father, the Tutankhamun of notebooks. An Aztec deity, perhaps. The Aztec deity of the notebook in the city's historic centre, along with some of the other stones that gave us our country: Idealnotl, green jade. The Green of Moctezuma's headdress, the green of the Mexican flag, Lorca's green how I love you green. Green like the top of the tree which is the headdress of the deity of paper. That single example, the pre-Hispanic god of everything small.

We haven't talked about it, but I'm not going to put up a Christmas tree. In your house, they did talk about it. Marina will buy the tree, and your dad will polish up the baubles your mum kept in the cupboard. They're in what used to be your room, in the third drawer down, Marina said to your dad. Although last year we didn't have a tree, this time I'd ask you, maybe you'd like us to have one. Can I tell you something? The other afternoon, walking along the pavement, I saw a woman putting up a Christmas tree in her living room. I could see her from head to foot through the large window. A woman alone, hanging coloured baubles on a plastic pine tree. I felt a longing to be living that life, a longing to be her. Why? I imagined two people talking about their day, the little bulbs flashing on and off, on and off. So far from our reality. Like a story I'd have liked to visit with you today.

The power's just gone. I lit the candles you bought the last time there was a blackout. Six little candles on the table. Let's hope the power comes back soon, because it looks like the notebook's holding a spiritualist meeting, only without the paranormal effects.

19

Last night I met a young guy in a bar who was identical to Proust. Identical. I couldn't think of a good excuse to take a photo, but I chatted to him. He had a black eye. He said he'd been beaten up buying cocaine in the Doctores neighbourhood. Someone tried to mug him as he was leaving the building, and he wouldn't hand over his wallet and phone. 'I wasn't giving that stupid kid anything, and the fucker smacked me one because I didn't,' said the twenty-four-year-old Mexican Proust with the black eye. A sociology student at the university, from a family in which everyone has read Marx. 'Even my granddad's read Marx. So have I, obviously, but that's not the most hardcore thing I've ever done. You want to know what the most hardcore thing I've ever done is? Something I'm really fucking proud of. I read all seven volumes of *In Search of Lost Time*. All seven of the bastards, from start to finish. And you know what? Proust's the fucking *man*. A total dude. Every character, even the seriously unimportant ones, turns up again later in the books. And all of them, every single one of the fuckers, has a past, a family and a shitload of stories. Over the seven volumes you get millions of these endless scenes, packed with sentimental details. He's seriously sentimental, I'm telling you. All those characters are seriously sentimental. And just think, the whole crew from all seven volumes wouldn't even fit into this bar, let alone a club. There's fucking millions of them, I'm telling you. And another thing, they all have their dramas, their purpose, their part to play, they're not just hanging about for no reason. Plus the guy spends an insane number of pages on everything. He'll go on for fifty pages about any old crap. Proust, man, I'm telling you. He's a fucking dude.'

We chatted at the bar. Julia saw someone she knew and went to sit at their table. Proust's friends got bored by the conversation and went out to smoke. In the toilets, heady with the alcohol and the hallucination, I wondered if there'd ever been another young guy who looked so much like Proust. We swapped numbers. He said he was having a barbecue on his balcony the next weekend, that he lived with two friends he was sure I'd get on with – one girl who's a tattoo artist and another who's a poet from Chiapas – and that he wanted to invite me to the barbecue so we could talk more, because they, the people he was with, wanted to go to a party in the Narvarte neighbourhood. I kept his number and his name: Proust, twenty-four years old.

In Sweden, in Japan, in Holland, could there be a young woman identical to Clarice Lispector? A girl identical to Virginia Woolf on the streets of Palermo in Buenos Aires, or a young Jorge Luis Borges riding the tube in London? A teenager on a skateboard, listening to reggae, who's the spitting image of Ibsen?

Probably.

I ran into your friend Marcos. We talked about you, and about your dad and Marina. He told me your mum used to take you and Marina for bike rides in the park when you were children. I told him I've given up on counting the days, since they're all the same. Marcos said: 'It's good for Jonás to have you in his life. He's a gentleman, he never tells me the details of your relationship, but even though he's away, I can tell you he's a better person now. It's much better that you're with him than that you're not. I hope you stay together.'

Maybe there isn't another twenty-four-year-old Proust with a black eye in a bar. Maybe there isn't another Oscar Wilde in the supermarket queue. Maybe there isn't another Fernando Pessoa eating a slice of orange dusted with chilli, which the guy under the pink awning in the market offers him on the tip of a knife. But please let there be a teenager on a skateboard, listening to reggae, who's the spitting image of Ibsen.

In primary school, a teacher read us a story by Oscar Wilde. I read it again as soon as I got home. It was a story about a giant and it captivated me. And that night, something began. For my fourteenth birthday, my uncle, the husband of my aunt Eva, posted me a book of Fernando Pessoa's poems. Reading the first pages of the book, I forgot all about my party. My granddad asked me to come down for the cake. Later that night, in my bedroom with the light on, reading the book again, something began. So much has happened since I read those books for the first time. I disagree with so many of the things I've done and said since then, but some books are like dots that form a line. Maybe it's to do with books and doors being the same shape. Proust opened one for me when I was seventeen. A big door, I know. And something else happened that was equally big. At that age I discovered reggae and hip hop. It was that combination, and my skateboarding boyfriend, that showed me the cosmos.

It's time to say it: I love my slippers. Especially on a Friday night, like now. I think you can do everything in slippers: open doors, discover planets, travel the Milky Way. An armchair and slippers are just right for a cosmic voyage.

This morning I looked for Ideal notebooks in a stationer's near Parque México. They didn't have any, but I chatted for a bit with the Spaniard at the counter. He was listening to opera, and had a blunt pencil behind his ear. A faded Madrid accent, like the globes in the window that had faded in the sun. His shirt sleeves were rolled up, and a packet of Camels was wedged under his right cuff. A gruff voice, a fatherly tone. Dusty dissertations, styrofoam solar systems in dirty plastic bags, pens, pencils, abacuses. A stationery shop with the objects my brother and I used to buy all that time ago. Maps. Those maps he remembered he needed late one Sunday evening. All those objects that were once called 'classroom essentials' and now hardly seem essential at all. I liked that man and his stationery shop, so resistant to the passing of time, as if in denial about the present, listening to opera, enjoying his cigarette behind the counter, under a white light that gave character to the smoke. I asked him about Ideal notebooks; he said he knew of them but hadn't had any in stock for years. As if rummaging in the bottom of a drawer, he eventually remembered he had a red Ideal diary in his storeroom at home, left over from a set a while ago. If I wanted to come back during the week, he could bring it for me. 'For now, can I offer you a cigarette?' he asked in his solemn, gruff voice. Standing in that stationery shop, with that man, would have been an excellent time to take up smoking again.

See? I'm like the notebook detective. A whodunnit that opens with a blank notebook lying motionless on the floor.

You have to gather up the clues, solve the mystery of the twin notebook which lives, oblivious to the other's exploits, on a different continent. A thriller on a small scale. Everyday life where very little happens: the crime of the epic.

Today I realised: Parque México and Parque España are very close together. Walking from one park to the other, I felt like I was getting closer to you. The two parks are about four or five minutes apart, just a few blocks. That short distance, like the words that separate Iberian Spanish from Mexican Spanish. But I find it reassuring to know that someone this evening – a man on a bicycle, a woman pushing a child in a pram, a teenager on a skateboard – is connecting Parque México with Parque España, as if those journeys were silently connecting us.

I had dinner with Guillermo. At one point he said: 'Ah, yes, my twenty-four-year-old friend Proust, with the black eye.' I enjoyed hearing that, it was as if he'd given me a toffee. I never buy them, but I like it when people give them to me.

I dreamed Jonás was sick. My mother was looking after him. When I entered the scene, Jonás, lying in bed, was furious, and my mother, who had a little towel in her hand, was upset. I wanted to understand what had happened, but Jonás was saying something hurtful to my mother. She responded in kind, handed me the towel and left the room. I didn't recognise Jonás, there was even something strange about his voice. And my mother would never have reacted like that. They get on well, my mother's fond of Jonás. My whole family's fond of him. I woke up feeling like I was holding the towel, convinced I was a long way from reality. I thought the beach looked further away than before.

Am I getting closer or am I getting further away?

I saw the dwarf on my block going into the bakery. Well-dressed, as always, talking on the phone, picking up the metal tray and tongs in his other hand. The king of small things, the lord of everyday life, the hero of the notebook thriller. Him so elegant, and the bigger stories so badly dressed.

On the way home, I thought about him. Blind people develop sharper hearing; deaf people learn a sophisticated system of signs. There are ways of compensating for disabilities. Being a dwarf isn't a disability, and yet those centimetres that separate them from other people need to be compensated for. If the dwarf were tall, would he dress so elegantly? Perhaps the attention to detail in his outfits is like a kind of animal fur. Just as animals with no fur find a means of covering themselves, and animals that can't attack find a means of camouflage, and strong animals seek to kill, the small ones, those who live on a smaller scale, have detail as their weapon. The marble tip of the miniature cane of the dwarf on the block, for example.

The days all look so similar to one another, like waves. And so, if not through details, how else can daily life be defended?

Don't be alarmed if this isn't going anywhere. Don't expect theories, reliable facts or conclusions. Don't take any of this too seriously. That's what universities are for, and theses, and academic studies. Personally, I like cafés, bars and living rooms. Not to mention comfortable cushions. So nice and cosy.

I'm so much like the cat. Now, batting around a little ball with a bell inside. My little ball: what's the relationship between voices and silence? No, the bell isn't ringing yet. Let me try again. Is silence the absence of the voice? Maybe they're family, and silence is the mother of the word. And maybe the word, when it was born, was music and poetry at once. The day the birds sang. Something like the day the voice was born.

Today is Christmas. The city is empty, there's almost no one in the park. I went for a bike ride and cycled around it a few times. The winter light projects the treetops onto the ground; the leaves move in the breeze and their shadows move on the concrete. You could see it as a film where nothing happens. I rode around the park a few times, as if watching, over and over, the film of the leaves' shadows moving on the ground.

On the way home, a stranger smiled cheerily at me. It brightened up my afternoon.

Sometimes I miss talking to my granddad. What would he say about this? Am I getting closer or further away?

Sometimes I feel sure I'm getting further away.

But do these stairs go up or down?

I had a good time at dinner. We ate, we drank. I chatted to everyone. In the early hours, my brother and I booked flights to the beach for a few days. The sea, at last. Perhaps there I'll manage to work out if I'm getting closer or further away.

20

Tania on the phone: 'I feel so guilty, honestly. I've been sitting in this armchair all day. I read a few pages, watched a film and then fell asleep. Maybe I'll spend the rest of my life like this.'

A while ago, Jonás put the Beckett questionnaire to Antonio and Olivia when they came over for dinner. They're here on a visit now, I just met them for breakfast. They gave me three little stones their daughters found in the sea. One white, one grey and one black: 'When they brought us these stones, which look like sweets, we thought they'd be perfect for someone to keep in their pocket and suck on now and then, like a Beckett character.'

Carolina and I arranged to meet in a café to edit a text. The background music gradually took centre stage. At first it was annoying and we couldn't concentrate. After three or four songs, Carolina started to dance in her seat, moving with difficulty, holding onto her belly. She raised one hand, took off her glasses and said: 'This is great, it's the kind of song we should be dancing to at three in the morning, wasted.'

I don't know what having a child is like, but if this notebook were a dwarf planetary system, the planets' centre of gravity would be the mother. Jonás' mother who took him far away, my mother to whom I've got closer, my friend who's about to give birth, and us, the children. Including our parents and siblings, Jonás.

A shooting star: a mother taking out her anger on a taxi driver who insulted her recently-deceased mother.

The black hole: the mystery of femicides and violence against women.

A headline in today's paper: 'Daughter of journalist decapitated'.

What's your worst nightmare?

In the earliest nightmare I can remember, my mother's voice disappeared. It was fading, becoming impossible to hear. I was running through the forest, the supermarket or the park. The plot doesn't matter, the point is her voice was gone by the end. And what scale is that on, compared to a daughter who dies before her father?

Ernesto's parents lost a child before he was born, a cot death. In one of the most profound and beautiful conversations I had with his father after dinner, he said: 'A natural death, but if that's nature, then the cruelty of it really makes you think. How do you explain a child dying first? You never get over it. It's the worst possible tragedy and it shouldn't happen to anyone.'

Have we got used to cruelty?

Changes in the cabinet, a change of president and the numbers don't change. I wonder what would happen if each parent, each child, each person who's lost someone in the last few years picked up the microphone to talk about their loss, more or less like Ernesto's dad did at the table or like in the early hours of the morning when Jonás told me the details of his mother's death. Every single one of those stories out loud.

What are we doing?

Come on out of the whale's belly now, you can't escape. Come away with me.

We edited the text at Carolina's. She specialised in seventeenth-century literature at university and almost always has some surprise, some verse, some titbit of information or point of comparison that she offers up with a smile, as if she's telling you the time or paying you a compliment. It comes naturally to her, it's part of how her mind works. Last night she told me about Diego de Mexía's translation of the letter Penelope wrote to Odysseus: 'Since I used it in my thesis I know all the gossip. It's from 1608, and I think it's the best translation. The book has an incredible history. He was Peruvian and he did the translation for a project called *Antarctic Parnassus*, an anthology designed to present the best poets from his country in Spain. A kind of introduction of Peruvian literature to Spanish society. Translating Ovid for the motherland: a symbol of poetic validation. But the gossip, as always, is better. In the prologue, Diego de Mexía included a text called "Discourse in Praise of Poetry", which is pretty bad and very boring. Really crap, actually. An anonymous text that for a long time people thought was written by a woman. One of the final theories about that prologue is that it was written by Diego de Mexía pretending to be a woman, which makes sense because all the letters in the book were written by women; his and the ones by heroines of classical mythology. He was feeling very Ovidian, I think. Anyway, the translation is wonderful. Penelope's letter to Odysseus is a gem. Look, it's up there, if you stand on the stool and get the book down, I'll lend you a recent translation and the one by Diego de Mexía to compare.'

I found an interesting verse. I'm going to put pins through the two translations, although the second butterfly is the one that will decorate this living room. In the contemporary version: 'Love is a matter filled with worries and fears.' In Diego de Mexía's version: 'For love is ever filled with fear'.

The letters Greek heroines write to men who aren't there. Ovid imagines what a woman would say to a man who wasn't there. Ovid, *mon amour.* 'These words your Penelope sends to you, O Ulysses, slow of return that you are; writing back is pointless: come yourself!'

It's three fifty-two a.m. We went to a cantina, and then to Tania's house. Did Penelope masturbate while she waited for Odysseus? Because I've just taken off my shirt.

How can I know if it's love or the complication of love that attracts me?

The taxi's here. The doorbell made me jump, and I've forgotten how I was going to answer that last question.

In the airport bookshop I saw the cover of a book called *The Principle of Happy Families.* A typical stock image: a man giving a child a piggy-back, a woman leading a girl down the beach by the hand. All four are smiling. The smiles are obviously at the photographer's request. It's clear they're not blood relations.

There are a lot of children on this flight. The parents have a kind of camaraderie; they lend each other toys, share food, chat across the aisle. Perhaps in a different place this wouldn't happen. I wonder if these young couples, these families on their way to the beach, also long for a moment or a life like the cover of that book. Is that their idea of happiness? I'd like to know.

No, not really. They've just given me some savoury biscuits and I'm reading a really good book. I've learnt that Saint John of the Cross was so short that Saint Teresa of Ávila called him half a friar. Like Lautrec, whose short stature meant he introduced himself as 'half a bottle'. The dwarf on the block could be half a bottle of absinthe, especially when he wears a top hat.

There's a Mexican wrestler who has a sidekick, a dwarf in a colourful costume. That half-wrestler apes his companion's moves, like a kind of comical shadow. I feel like the worst of this country's political class are a comical shadow. A half-bureaucracy, a half-bottle unable to contain the violent sea.

21

We're on a beach near Tulum. We went for a long walk; I haven't had a conversation like that with my brother for ages. I'd really missed it. The sea, at once both deep and light, seems to encourage extremes. The sea that sinks ships and the sea that tosses a nappy on its surface is the same. The same as ever. And yet, there are no two identical combinations of waves or two identical moments. It's the repetition, like a ritual of waves. And that old melody in the background. Oh, I love how its whistling messes up my hair.

We talked about Jonás, and Ana, and our friends. About his girlfriend and the problems they're having. About work, about the things we'd like to do. We remembered a trip to the beach when we were children. We talked about some things I remember, and some things he remembers, as if we were playing cards. I told him, in detail, about the accident. He told me, in detail, how it was for him, being so far away, the phone calls to our parents, what was going through his head. We cried on the beach, and we laughed, then we went to a palm-roofed shack for some beers.

I love what Shakespeare wrote from the point-of-view of the sea: 'A hundred thousand welcomes! I could weep, And I could laugh; I am light, and heavy. Welcome!'

The sea is the most musical of landscapes.

Walking along the beach last night, my brother said he'd turn into a fish because he likes swimming. I'd rather turn into a bird, so I could sing as I look down at the waves.

I wish you were here, Jonás.
I wish you were here.
I wish.
I weave.
I unravel.

Am I getting closer or am I getting further away?

I realise how good it is to reach the bottom. Accidentally or on purpose. Down where the ship sinks, down where there's no light. Where it's cold and dark, and there are only words. Then emerging, seeing the nappy tossed this way and that on the surf. A nappy or anything else that sullies the expanse. A reminder. A Post-it for the ordinary. Like one nurse singing a Shakira song to another. Or the bell for the rubbish truck announcing its arrival, so you hurry to tie a knot in the plastic bag or do whatever else reminds you how good it is to be on the surface. Being here is so good.

Shall we do a crossword or do you want to play cards with us?

I didn't tell you, but one advantage of the ideal notebook is that it can record the sound of the sea, so you can listen when you get back.

That ebb and flow.

Listen, I want to tell you something. There was once a sea that was horrible in the daytime and beautiful at night. The wind was confused. It didn't understand why, if it always blew in more or less the same direction, the sea could be horrible and beautiful on the same day. Perhaps what's horrible can also be beautiful, thought the wind.

Perhaps what's horrible is also beautiful, Jonás.

Then what could pain turn into?

Maybe the same stairs that go down also go up.

22

Back at work, back at home and back to writing in pencil. I've realised that some pens bring out the worst defects of handwriting, and others emphasise the best. A pencil, however, shows the writing for what it is, with no filters, as if lit by natural light. But the notebook seems to argue in favour of the pen, as if the pencil were making it uncomfortable, as if the blue lines were supposed to be the background. The lines and the pencil have the same tone, neither of the two stands out. The notebook, unconvinced, seems to say: 'Let the pens come unto me, for theirs is the kingdom of permanence.'

And so the notebook proverbs begin.

The word was brought forth when there were no depths, when there were no fountains abounding with water; before the mountains were settled, before the hills were formed, before the day and the starry night, the word was brought forth. And so, notebooks, hearken unto it, for blessed are those that keep words.

And so the cedar and gold doors to the ideal notebook's proverb collection swing open.

Pencils and fountain pens can be erased, but biros last forever.

When the whirlwind passes by, the story is no more, but gossip has an everlasting foundation.

Those who speak on the phone grow tired of themselves; those who tell stories escape themselves.

Those who talk too much reject themselves; those who listen carefully accept themselves.

The beginning of a story fears and departs from mistakes, but the end is arrogant and self-confident.

The story is brought down by its mistakes, but publication shelters them in the passage of time.

Planning is an abomination to the omniscient narrator, and improvising is her delight.

The man in a suit walks to work, but the omniscient narrator describes him.

The omniscient narrator's wrath is a premonition of death, but the minor character can soothe it.

The pursuit of literary fame comes before disaster, and texts are its flames.

Literary fame will be diminished, whereas one word after another will increase.

The writer's silver-haired head is a crown found in the way of readings; so is the writer's alopecia, but for halitosis there is no excuse.

A friend loves at all times, but some phrases are born for adversity.

Seek words, and there are none; no longer seek them and they shall come.

The bad writer says 'There is a critic outside! I shall be slain in the streets!' because he thinks he deserves attention.

'It is good for nothing!' says the young critic. But when he has gone on his way, then he embraces himself.

Better to dwell in the wilderness than with a writer in receipt of a grant.

The first person hates heavy things, because she has to carry all the pages; meanwhile, the omniscient narrator loves long stories because they show off her strength.

Disorder is the nature of stories, but an orderly bookshelf is the honour of booksellers.

The minor character thinks his behaviour is notable, but the omniscient narrator barely mentions his name.

All stories are a deep ocean and a puddle at the same time.

23

The word, then, contains both the real and the imaginary in equal amounts. The word pulls you to the bottom and lets you swim comfortably on the surface. The word can be a sea or a puddle. Phrases can contain anything, like these delicious coconut biscuits I'm eating.

As I dip a coconut biscuit in my coffee, I see Odysseus is in despair because he can't get out: 'now I've crossed this waste of water, the end in sight, there's no way out of the boiling surf – I see no way!'

So we still don't know how to swim diagonally.

Did I tell you I've never had an electric pencil sharpener? As a girl I thought they were like a symbol of adult life. There was one on my father's desk and one on my teacher's desk. One of those emblematic objects from the world I didn't belong to, the world of things that were too sharp or too heavy or too high. Like the flag of another country, where there were different objects, a different language, a different system. The foreign country of adult life. Mine was the world of flat things, plastic things that didn't break, cheap things like the pencil sharpener I had. Manageable on my scale, now so distant in time. I never had an electric pencil sharpener but, like a sailor with an anchor tattoo, I could tattoo a blue pencil sharpener onto my arm. The anchor to a past which now seems made up.

Do you realise the pencil sharpener is like a nappy you lose sight of in the waves, which then suddenly pops up somewhere else?

We're getting nautical now, so Bartolomé de las Casas enters the scene, picks up the microphone, taps it a few times and then announces who the star navigator was in days gone by: 'Juan de la Cosa, from Biscay, the best pilot there ever was on those seas.'

Poseidon worked against Odysseus. He prevented his passage, whipped the sea into a frenzy, shipwrecked him time and again. Odysseus could be seen as a mediocre sailor because it took him ten years to get home. In contrast, Juan de la Cosa travelled with Christopher Columbus. On returning to Cadiz, Juan de la Cosa produced a map of the world for the Catholic Monarchs; the oldest map to feature the American continent. There's an inscription in the margin: 'Made by Juan de la Cosa in the Port of Santa María in the year 1500'.

Juan de la Cosa put Latin America on the map for the first time.

Tania on the phone: 'But wait, the coolest thing is that you can't tell what's sea and what's land on Juan de la Cosa's map.'

The sea and the land get mixed up. Juan de la Cosa left an inconclusive ending, opening his map up to double readings: the sea merges with the land and we don't know if the continent continues. The mother of all ambivalences, which is also the mother of us.

Cuba is clearly shown as an island. Christopher Columbus described arriving in Cuba, and Severo Sarduy says in an interview that Christopher Columbus began Cuban literature when he described the birdsong before anything else. That's how Sarduy explains the musicality of the speech, of the poetry in Cuba. In other words, the literary history of Latin America began not with text but with birdsong.

Oh, I just love that Juan de la Cosa has the word *cosa* in his name. Juan of the Thing. It's like a present I don't want to open. What thing is it? Is the Thing something like the mother of all things? The man who put the American continent on the map was called Of the Thing.

Tania on the phone: 'You know, Juan de la Cosa could be the patron saint of artists.'

The music makes the ambivalence bearable. Not knowing if it's land or sea. Not knowing if it carries on or stops. Not knowing if I'm swimming onwards or getting further away. But the music is so good.

Did I tell you I saw a waiter with a swallow tattooed on his arm? I asked him why he'd got that tattoo and he said he searched for 'tattoos' online and it was one of the first designs he saw in the results. Guillermo, tracing circles with his finger around the rim of his whisky glass, said when the waiter had left: 'I once read that sailors had tattoos of birds because they were a sign land was near.'

Did Juan de la Cosa have any tattoos?

Miguel de Cervantes put the novel in Spanish on the map. Sor Juana Inés de la Cruz put New Spain on the map. Cervantes and Sor Juana put the language on the map. The map to which Borges gave so many names. But we can't sanctify the map, we have to get it dirty, toss in a nappy, a fizzy-drink bottle, a plastic bag. The map of the language is spacious and has room for infomercials, the latest literary releases and the day's terrible news. Words live together as equals on that map.

The Word continues to be real and imaginary in equal amounts. The Thing could be real or imaginary. The word and the thing are ambivalent, like the land and the sea on the map from 1500.

Penelope has something of Odysseus about her. Odysseus has something of Penelope. The roles in a relationship tend to go back and forth, to swap over. The bed, that site of domestic ambivalence.

Am I getting closer or am I getting further away?

A text message. Carolina has just given birth.

This morning, we talked about the text we edited. At one point she said she misses smoking, that she associates editing with smoking: 'And just think, in the old days we'd go out and buy cigarettes no matter what time it was. Do you think your niece Lila will ever nag anyone the way I used to nag you to go to the corner shop?'

You know what, Lila? I think we need another map which marks the corner shops, stationers', hairdressers', little restaurants and independent businesses in this city. I'd give you the map as a present. I could make a fake biography of Juan of the Useless Thing. His achievements would be as useless and extravagant as his hat. Juan of the Useless Thing would show you the map of the corner shops, stationers', hairdressers' and places like that, and all the unofficial, makeshift businesses that constitute day-to-day life in this city, to welcome you.

24

Jonás is coming back soon.

I found an A4 Ideal notebook in the city centre. This notebook is about to run out. Maybe I won't use the next one, because it's very big and Jonás will be back soon. It feels important to add that I still haven't found a notebook like this one, a triplet for our pair.

Just as love songs are all alike, gossip magazines are all alike and waiting rooms are all alike. Instead of making us unique, waiting makes us ordinary. And a wait for a lover is the most ordinary kind. Maybe that's its appeal.

I saw the dwarf from my block at the supermarket. He was wearing a navy-blue three-piece suit and holding hands with his daughter, a little girl. They were in the queue next to mine, the queue for fifteen items or fewer. He had a litre of milk in one hand, and his other hand was holding the girl's. She was wearing pink pyjamas, a red sweater and white shoes. I remembered something, and it struck me that a mystery was being solved. One time when we had an argument, before you went away, I saw the dwarf in the street with a cane. I felt like him, like I needed a cane myself. I don't know why I thought he was single, but in fact the dwarf on the block has a beautiful diminutive daughter who goes shopping with him in pyjamas. The girl asked him to buy her a chocolate, and he did, affectionately, letting go of her hand to pick up a chocolate bunny rabbit wrapped in gold foil. I felt like I was seeing something I hadn't known about in that action, a side I hadn't imagined, a scene that seemed to ground him in the here and now. The elegant, solemn man, who looks like he's from another era, the man who some time ago smiled at me in the street with an almost novelistic air about him, was the same man who was passing a chocolate bunny rabbit to his daughter.

The dwarf's navy-blue suit, the same colour as the sweater I had in my plastic pencil sharpener days. A sweater printed with the face of an English soldier, the classic helmet covering more than half of his face, leaving only his mouth in view. My father at the wheel of the beige Beetle. The white, red and yellow lights in the streets. Sharp pinpricks of colour in the sky, stripes of light flashing past at speed. The music he hummed, as if singing would expose him too much. I bought a chocolate bunny rabbit for my father.

The health of my uncle, my father's brother, is declining rapidly. He told me when I called just now to invite him for dinner.

Jonás usually wears plain cotton T-shirts and shirts. His T-shirts are navy blue, white and grey, and some are stripy. Since he left, I've been using his T-shirts as pyjamas. Although we're more or less the same size, my clothes don't fit him. And I've been waiting so long to take yours off you, Jonás. I wish we could have one of those Saturdays of getting up at one p.m., eating in the Japanese restaurant then going back home again. Oh, the smell of the bed on a Saturday evening.

I have three words, three tiny stones to suck: come back, Jonás.

That plea is what ends Penelope's letter to Odysseus, as imagined by Ovid. But I'm still here, in this waiting room. Did I tell you I like artificial plants? Maybe I should buy one for the house, like a souvenir of this journey, a reminder, a Post-it note. I still haven't left and something good has just happened, I've just found a magazine with a horoscope from three years ago.

Maybe it's not about swimming diagonally. Maybe it's about floating, parting my hair at the side, combing my fringe to the right and now the left, sweeping my hair back, pretending I'm moving forwards and ending up in the same place. If being here is so nice, why do I need to get there?

I'm restyling my hair while it's wet. And I move my left shoulder up and then down again. I lift my right shoulder and lower it. I stretch out an arm, stretch out the other. One, two three. I move my arms up and down, one, two, three, one, two, three. It looks like I'm dancing.

The Wizard of Oz is so insipid behind his shower curtain. A real let-down. But then, isn't the yellow-brick road what makes it all worthwhile? Are the blue lines of the notebook like the tiles of the blue-brick road? If so, you know what song David Bowie could sing at the end of this film.

And so, like the line in that Simone Weil book, seawater can be life-sustaining for fish and deadly for humans. That ambivalence makes the blue-brick road more appealing.

Oh, I just love being here. I'm not moving forwards, I'm floating. And floating is so different when you've lost your fear of drowning. Unhappy are those who remain within their grief, when the here and now is so good. Although, you know what? I could leave any minute, Jonás. But, look, here I am. It's easier to do my hair when it's wet. I'm going to part it in the middle to welcome you back, listen: 'A hundred thousand welcomes! I could weep, and I could laugh; I am light, and heavy. Welcome!'

Suddenly I think about that Shakira song. Such a good reminder of the here and now.

I go from the office to the apartment, the study to the kitchen, the kitchen to the table, the chair to the armchair. These are more or less my routes, my routine. But it doesn't feel like I'm here in the study, with the cat asleep in the armchair; it feels like I'm somewhere else.

From the right for a moment,

and from the left for a change.

Here on this page. But also here, without knowing what's next, without it mattering what's next.

Sometimes I remember who I used to be. I feel like I was a different person before the accident, like I might be two people shaking hands when they're introduced. I did so many things and said so many things in the name of fear. Fear of something changing. As if I didn't want anything to change, as if I wanted the horoscope to be valid for another month, another year, another lifetime. For Monday to be the same as Tuesday, for Thursday to be the same as next Thursday and for the phrases, like the days, to come round again.

Oh, the need to retain. Being anal. The anus dominates empires. Like fear. Fear of loss. Fear of loving and being loved. Fear of listening and being heard. Come here, Ovid: 'For love is ever filled with fear'.

It feels so good to let go and be here. Here and now. In the moment.

Change. Unlearning yourself is more important than knowing yourself.

My dad rings the bell. Time to go for dinner. I'll give him the chocolate bunny rabbit I bought.

I dreamed I was asleep. In the bedroom, alone, on my side of the bed, which is the side where I've slept since Jonás went to Spain. The moonlight was streaming in through the big window, just like before I dozed off. A presence, a gaze that awoke me. Part of the dream, of course. A dwarf at the foot of the bed, looking at me. It wasn't the dwarf on my block. It was a stranger who didn't seem to mean me any harm, but nevertheless I was afraid. I made a face that asked him what he was doing there. 'Come,' he said, in a kind voice. 'Don't be afraid, I'm here to show you the future.' I got out of bed and he told me to open the curtain on the small window, which I remember having closed before going to sleep. I drew back the curtain and saw a child crawling along with his back to me, in the direction of a tree. Before seeing his face, before the child turned around, just before he called me mummy, I woke up.

'It hadn't occurred to me before, but what if I'm afraid of the future?' I asked Julia over the phone. Now I don't think I am. In the dream I wasn't scared to pull back the curtain. And, like in the dream, I'm not interested in seeing the face of what's to come. Here I am, Jonás. The bell for the rubbish truck is ringing and we really need to take out the bags.

25

Tepepunk and Nina are back from Japan. We stayed up chatting until late. It turns out that Catalina, the art collector Tania told me about a while ago, has bought one of Tepepunk's pieces. On Friday she's hosting a dinner party at her house so she can meet them. They've invited me along.

Tepepunk pulled the bell cord. A man in jeans and a white shirt opened the door and led us through the garden to a small room. Catalina was sitting in an armchair between two tall, handsome teenagers with curly hair, who looked around fifteen or sixteen years old. 'My friend Vico's children,' said Catalina. Without moving from the armchair, she introduced herself as Catalina, looking at Tepepunk, seemingly unaware that Nina and I were there.

Catalina, in her seventies, had short, wavy, completely white hair swept to one side with a tortoiseshell comb. Pearl earrings and a little tight-fitting black dress with long sleeves. She rose to pick up a bell. On her feet, she was level with my shoulders, a woman small in stature. Tiny, in fact. A well-proportioned body, a beautiful face. I thought she was attractive, elegant. She invited us to sit down. Switching between Italian and Spanish, she mainly addressed her friend's children and Tepepunk. She asked him some questions about his return to Mexico, about the residency in Tokyo, and asked him to say more when her friend Vico arrived, since he'd once been a cultural attaché in Japan.

'And are you Mexican?' Catalina asked me. She'd taken a piece of crystallised orange peel from a dainty plate and was pointing it in my direction. It didn't seem to matter whether I answered the question or not; waving the orange peel at me was her way of acknowledging my presence in the room. She asked Nina the same thing, pointing at her with the peel from which she'd just taken a bite.

The room, unlike her behaviour, was very welcoming. There were recognisable artworks: a Dr. Atl, a Baldessari, a Ruelas, a sketch by Frida Kahlo. Some old hand-coloured photos. White armchairs, a heavy wooden table in the centre. An upright piano, and some antiques on a little table between Nina and me. A wooden radio, a pendulum clock, a metronome, a pair of binoculars and a bronze rhinoceros. The background music made our exclusion less awkward.

Each object seemed to be there to tell the story of some journey, event or family achievement. An Italian relative who survived a fire, perhaps, and that bronze rhinoceros was one of the few things found in the rubble. An uncle playing that piano, to the rhythm of that metronome, in the first silent screenings in a cinema in Rome. A cousin in Tuscany humming the love songs she heard on the radio that no longer works. Everything there seemed to have the sole purpose of allowing Catalina to talk about her past.

'The bathroom, like almost all bathrooms, is at the back and to the left,' she answered, without looking at me. She offered some orange peel to the young men, who were lounging like lazy cats, as if they'd grown up among panthers. On the way to the bathroom I saw, in the darkness, two rooms decorated in different styles. One Persian and one French. The bathroom was quite big, with antique furniture. A hand-painted screen surrounded the toilet. Even the soap I used to wash my hands seemed to have a story, a history. It had the scent of another era, as if a family had made the soap for Catalina just like they made them in her childhood in Italy.

Nina made a face at me, as if to say, 'What are we doing here?' Catalina was holding forth to her friend's children and Tepepunk, and still avoiding the two of us. A woman who can't stand the presence of other women, her behaviour seemed to suggest. But at the same time, she was talking to them as if she wanted the two of us to look at her and take her in, as if she were displaying her plumage: 'Such a shame, boys, that you never saw New York in our day. Now *that* was nightlife, nothing like now. We've still got the apartment, you can go with your father whenever you like, but there's no real nightlife any more. When I was there, you wouldn't catch anyone getting up before noon. Anything interesting began at two in the morning.'

I looked at her tiny, well-manicured hands, her slender fingers, her discreet gold ring, as she began to weave names and stories together, addressing Tepepunk all the while. Federico Fellini, Coco Chanel, Picasso: 'Like that magnificent paella Buñuel made at his house in Del Valle, not to mention the pasta my dear Federico taught me to make in Roma. Not many people know this, but Federico was an excellent cook, he could put any chef in this city to shame. And just think, his forte was still making films.'

Vico, the young men's father, came in with a brown paper bag. 'You won't believe the wine I found, my dear,' and then he said something in Italian as he wiped his shoes on the mat by the door. The rest of us moved into the dining room. The three of us exchanged glances, and made a whispered plan to go for a drink when we left.

Catalina came in with a glass of red wine. Vico poured some for us, and Catalina went to the far end of the dining room to put on some music. I'd given up hope of interacting with her; I was looking at a drawing when she walked past and murmured: 'Picasso was good in bed, but that drawing he dashed off in five minutes is better than any story I could tell you.' She carried on by, sat at the head of the table and summoned the cook with a little bell.

26

Tania on the phone: 'No, forget Picasso, you want some real gossip? At the party last night, the Most Important Artist in Mexico seriously overdid it. Marcelito was so drunk he broke the sink in the bathroom, imagine. And Natalia slept with Manuel. She said it was a bad idea. Unbelievable, right? She told me herself, I ran into her just now buying a coffee. She's not embarrassed – if you see her having breakfast, pull up a chair and she'll tell you everything that happened last night. I have the feeling that if she'd seen a film, she would have quoted some of the dialogue for me. I think the way she is matches her work, I like that about her.'

I called in to see Carolina and Lila this afternoon. I wanted to tell her about the visit to Catalina's house, especially the conversation we had after dinner. 'I'd love to meet her,' Carolina said, putting a bonnet on her daughter. 'The number of stories that woman has must make her one of the best gossip anthologies of the twentieth century,' she added, trying to breastfeed, while the baby was falling asleep. 'I think there's another woman, an Englishwoman who was also friends with Duchamp, living in Mexico City as well. I know he and Catalina were friends towards the end. Last year I published a book and learnt a bit about it. Apparently one of Catalina's projects is restoring a rented room in

Buenos Aires where Duchamp lived for nine months. There was a time in Duchamp's life when he shaved his head completely, and I found out that the year Duchamp shaved his head was down to his stay in that room. He caught lice and got an infection that didn't go away for ages. And it gets juicier: did you know he wore wigs? His passion for wearing wigs and the invention of his female pseudonym Rrose Selavy – which in French, phonetically, means something incredible, *life is pink*, and which also involved a fictitious gender-bending – emerged from that time in Buenos Aires. His heartthrob hairstyle, slicked back like Carlos Gardel's, was always iconic, so his bald phase is a pretty big deal. I also know that during his time in Argentina, Duchamp joined a chess club. He spent his evenings reading books about chess, studying techniques. You wouldn't believe how seriously he took it. It was almost like another of his artworks: he saw the game as an extremely serious business, and meanwhile his art seemed more like a game. And one of those games began in Buenos Aires. Catalina must know a lot more about it. She's the one who wants to do something with that space, but I never found out if she bought it or not. I'd love to meet her, but she has a reputation for being a total bitch. And is it true she brings up her aristocratic heritage at every opportunity?'

There's something I forgot to mention. The same man who let us in showed us out via the back door, which opened onto a different street. Before leaving, I saw one of Catalina's cars. A cream-coloured Beetle. When I was little I used to like sleeping on the back seat, because the engine was at the back of the car and it made the seat nice and warm, plus riding in the car was a good opportunity to chat to my dad until I dozed off. My parents didn't keep that car. Catalina has the same one, in the same colour. I haven't seen that model since I was a girl, with those interiors, that same mixture of smells. How strange to see something in real life that looks just like a childhood memory. I felt as if that car could have belonged to my parents, or as if the car from the blue pencil sharpener days and Catalina's car were two dots along a line that was illegible to me, or as if that Beetle were an incoherent sign or a piece of this goddamn jigsaw puzzle that gets harder and harder to solve.

27

After dinner, Catalina had us move through into another room. A baroque altarpiece, some pre-Hispanic masks on a wooden table and a selection of works by young artists. The younger of the teenagers sat on a quartz chair shaped like a hand. Catalina told him it would do him good at his age: 'It will align your chakras, my dearest, so make yourself comfortable.' The cook came in with a china tea set, a little plate of orange peel, a sugar bowl and some tiny pincers which Catalina used to distribute sugar cubes. I said I didn't want any, but she offered again, as if she were interested less in sugar than in conversation. With me?

'Come on, we'll put some music on.' She strode ahead, leading me towards a wooden cabinet at the far end of the room. She asked me to open the doors carefully, because the cabinet had sentimental value. Knowing her, I thought, the wood could have come from one of the first guillotines. 'What kind of music do you listen to?' she asked. She wasn't impressed by my vague response, but I was interested less in finding shared tastes than in testing the surface of that frozen lake which seemed about to crack with every step. 'I was expecting a more convincing answer from you,' she said, removing a record from its sleeve. Catalina chose a *bolero*. At that point she was turned away from me, looking at the altarpiece, moving one shoulder in time to the music, singing under her breath, then moving the other shoulder, in circles. Singing, moving her left shoulder, then her right. She was humming, moving one hand, as if following the music, then moving the other, in time, when she asked:

'Do you know this song?'

'Yes.'

'Have you listened to it carefully?'

'It's a love song.'

'You're wrong. I'm a widow, and love's not the same for me as it is for someone young. This song is about someone for whom love *itself* has died. A loss for you young people is different, young people will end a relationship over any stupid thing. You don't understand, you're young. If this song were sung by a teenager, it would sound hollow. I bet you yourself believe there's no one else like him, as the song says. Do you have a boyfriend, are you married?'

'I have a boyfriend, we live together.'

'Why didn't you bring him?'

'He's away travelling, in Spain, but he's coming back this Sunday, the day after tomorrow.'

'What did he go to Spain for?'

'His mother died. He went with his family and decided to stay longer.'

'Searching for his mother. I see. And it's possible he's coming back to look for her in you. Well, as long as you don't take it into the bedroom you can be together.'

'What do you mean?'

'Precisely that. When he comes back, make sure you don't end up with a role that's not yours. If you want to have children, you will, in time, but don't let them be – what's his name?'

'Jonás.'

'My Ricardo lost his mother when we were dating. He was always very charismatic, an extrovert, the life

174

and soul, but something deep inside him hardened after that. The event marked his work, it changed it radically. Around that time we had Antonella, another extrovert, outgoing like her father. Ricardo was very close to *la mamma*. He was born on Calle Alfonso Reyes, and he wanted us to buy a house near where he was born. See what I mean? The problem is when you take that into the bedroom. Tell me, what does he do?'

'He's a mathematician, he's working on a research project. And he likes playing the piano.'

'Sensitive, intelligent, all that must really turn you on. But watch out: you're not going to save him.'

'I'm not trying to save him.'

'Are you sure? Personally, the only thing I'm sure of is that time brings more questions than answers. Sometimes it takes years to formulate a basic, fundamental question. This boy lost his mother. I lost mine at the age of eight, it was different for me than for Ricardo, but people are always trying to get close to *la mamma*, no matter how old they are. That doesn't change, he'll still be looking for her when he gets back. It's essential to understand that. You'll need to see, above all, what isn't on show. I'm going to lend you a book, it'll come in useful at this point, trust me. I prefer having my back to the street, as you've probably noticed. I'd rather look at any one of these works of art than the street, but then, unless it can show us reality in a different light, what's art for? You know where I live, bring it back after that Jonás of yours returns.'

28

My mum sent me this email: 'My darling daughter, you don't know how much I love you, how much I think about you. Yesterday I went to the clinic for a check-up, I was chatting to the doctor and I thanked him for looking after you. But silently, dear, I also said thank you because you're ok, and not only that but I can see you more clearly now. It's Friday night, I'm feeling calm and happy, and I wanted to tell you that I love you like I never believed possible, that what a son or daughter awakens in you is very powerful, and all the more so when they mean everything to you, the way you both do to me. Oh, and the doctor says you should go in and see them because he's got a new repertoire of jokes. He also said Jonás must be a very lucky man. Why don't you two come over when he's back? We'd like to know how he got on in Spain.'

29

Marina called when I was at Catalina's. Since her brother gets back tomorrow, she said, her dad wants to give me some things he picked up in the supermarket with us in mind. She's also bought some plants for their house, and has one for our apartment. I was in the car on the way home, listening to the radio, flicking between stations, when I heard this: 'I'm Rosa María Hernández, I'm thirty-five years old and I come from Chihuahua. I'm here to represent the other families who couldn't be here and the ones who are here behind me now. At this meeting, I want to ask you some questions, Mr President, because I want to know how you're going to restore peace to this country. My fifteen-year-old daughter Renata was murdered in the early hours of March 29th last year and I want to ask you, sir, what would you do if one of your children was tortured and killed? Tell me, what are you going to do to reduce impunity in the judicial system? How would you feel, sir, if you arrived at the Public Ministry seeking justice for your baby girl, and the authorities took no notice because they were busy with other things? I got a phone call that said come and identify your daughter. And how would you feel if the authorities said shush, madam, stop shouting, stop crying, go home quietly because sobbing here won't change anything? They tried to say my Renata was mixed up in bad things, but my husband, her brothers and sisters, and

God and I know she wasn't, we know my Renata didn't do anything wrong. My Renata was fifteen years old, she was at secondary school, my daughter was a good girl. Ever since they killed her my life's been hell, like the hell so many mothers here are going through. I've begged, I've cried everywhere, I've asked for help and never, ever been given any. I went to ask the governor for help, but he didn't even deign to open the door, and he's not answering my calls, either. Who's going to give us an explanation? Will my daughter Renata's killer go unpunished? Will the more than ninety thousand recorded deaths in recent years go unpunished? Will you deign to answer us or are you going to shut the door like all the other politicians? Any action you intend to take, don't forget that first you have to resolve the cases from the past and don't forget it's not just me asking for this, we're all asking for it, all of us who've lost our children, we're asking from the bottom of our hearts and with all the pain in our souls, because losing a child is the most painful thing there is, more painful even than our own death because we wish we'd been taken in their place.'

30

The book Catalina lent me is called *Classifying the Thousand Longest Rivers in the World*. Boetti and his wife, Annie Marie Sauzeau, took seven years to complete the project, and the book was published in 1977. The rivers contained within its red covers are ordered from longest to shortest. It begins with the Nile-Kagera, which is 6,671 kilometres in length. Some rivers meet along the way, like characters, and others, like pedestrians in different cities, never cross paths. It ends with the Agusan River, which is 384 kilometres long. All the rivers flow into the sea.

Rivers have a source, a life, a youth, an old age. Some have longer trajectories than others; some are abruptly cut off, while others follow a peaceful path to the end. The book only classifies the longest rivers. A grey box describes each one: its name, where it begins, where it ends and how long it is. Footnotes at the bottom of each page give the sources consulted, along with other measurements. Comparing one river to another, you see how slight the differences are in their lengths. In other words, it's obviously impossible to classify them exactly. That desire to classify them, like the desire to write accurately about the past, is based on a fiction. The book of rivers is like a silent novel. The trajectories are so similar despite being in different places, and yet the rivers, ordered from biggest to smallest, lie side by side. Impossibly side by side. They may not all meet along the way, but all the rivers are part of the same book.

Do stories, like rivers, all flow into the same place?

After the first sentences spoken by the woman on the radio, I parked so I could listen to her properly. I cried. I went and walked around a nearby park, I sat down by a tree. I cried for my parents, I cried for them both. I cried when I relived the accident and when I relived the nights that followed. I remembered the hell, the sweat, the smell. I cried for those nights when it seemed as if everything was beginning again. I cried for Ana's death. I cried because Jonás wasn't with me. I cried for that woman's story, for the situation she's in, which is the situation we're all in. I cried for the situation as a whole and maybe I also cried for the day I was born.

I wonder if stories can be classified like rivers, from biggest to smallest. I also wonder if, in that case, stories could be part of the same book. Passages placed impossibly side by side. So they make another story.

It's a good thing you're coming back tonight, Jonás. The black cat and I want night to fall so you'll arrive. What a strange life we lead day to day, and what a good thing you'll be here soon.

I haven't yet said that Guillermo gave me *My Friends* by Emmanuel Bove this week, the book I've been trying to track down for so long. It's not the first time Guillermo's given me a book I really care about, he's given me so many, but this one arrived at the perfect moment. I read it in a night. It was a nice surprise. At one point, Victor,